I0679922

SAVANNAH
SEAS
MAIDEN VOYAGE

CYNTHIA MANION

MVHL

Copyright © 2023 by Cynthia Manion

SAVANNAH SEAS
MAIDEN VOYAGE

All rights reserved. No part of this publication may be reproduced, distributed, or transmitted in any form or by any means, including photocopying, recording, or other electronic or mechanical methods, without the prior written permission of the publisher, except in the case of brief quotations embodied in critical reviews and certain other noncommercial uses permitted by copyright law.
For permission requests, write to the publisher, addressed "Attention: Permissions Coordinator"
carol@markvictorhansenlibrary.com

Quantity sales special discounts are available on quantity purchases by corporations, associations, and others. For details, contact the publisher at carol@markvictorhansenlibrary.com

Orders by U.S. trade bookstores and wholesalers.
Email: carol@markvictorhansenlibrary.com

Creative contribution by Amy Keane and Marylou Ambrose
Cover Design - Low & Joe Creative, Brea, CA 92821
Book Layout - DBree, StoneBear Design

Manufactured and printed in the United States of America distributed globally by markvictorhansenlibrary.com

New York | Los Angeles | London | Sydney

ISBN: 979-8-88581-116-3 Hardback
ISBN: 979-8-88581-117-0 Paperback
ISBN: 979-8-88581-118-7 eBook
Library of Congress Control Number: 2023916337

SAVANNAH SEAS
NEWEST MEMBER OF THE SAVANNAH VALLEY SERIES

Everyone imagines what life would be like living on an oceangoing super yacht. Who would you meet? What amazing places would you visit? Perhaps you know someone who took an ocean voyage and swore it was the best thing they ever did. Here's your chance to start the adventure in the *Savannah Seas Maiden Voyage*.

The characters in these books celebrate life and retirement in fun and imaginative ways after facing unexpected challenges. Here, new friendships are made, new horizons open, and a lifetime of experience and acquired wealth is celebrated.

Each book in the series is inspired by true events unique to each author. Sit back, relax, and allow yourself to be transported to the glorious and prestigious retirement vacation known as Savannah Seas.

TESTIMONIALS

"WOW! *Savannah Seas* by Cynthia Manion is a roller-coaster! Tabitha's on this crazy-luxury ship and just when you're getting comfy with the views, BAM, mystery hits. You won't want to put this one down. Grab some snacks, find a cozy spot, and dive in. It's a ride from start to finish!"

— Ken Walls, *#1 Bestselling Author and CEO*

"Here is your ticket to some life experiences that few can truly imagine. Take a cruise in the yachting world with *Savannah Seas*."

— Jim Cathcart, Hall of Fame Speaker and author of *Relationship Selling* plus 24 other books.

"*Savannah Seas* is full of delightful word / life pictures and phrases that took me on a journey that I might never make in real life. This fiction book seems so real and it's clean, easy to read, and fun with an undercurrent and meaning for the reader. I hope this is just the first in a series because I want to know more about this interesting group of people."

— Jay Skinner, *PDT Associates LLC, The CEO Extender / The Plastic Pallet Guy*

"The characters in *Savannah Seas* come alive in a beautiful story of adventure, finding your purpose, and above all, friendship. I highly recommend taking the leap and diving into *Savannah Seas* – you won't want to put it down!"
— Eric Rodriguez, *Founder of Headwater*

"*Savannah Seas* is a billionaire book; about billionaires, ne'er-do-wells, and billionaire customers, willing to put their money where their pride is. Cynthia Manion employs classic plot twists that you will love. And triumphs that you will celebrate. Great book. Great read."
— Jeffrey Gitomer, Author, *The Little Red Book of Selling: 12/5 Principles of Sales Greatness*

"What a delightful read *Savannah Seas* is. Enjoy a cruise, a new appreciation for life, all while traveling around the world making lifelong friends. Remember to empower yourself by taking time for you every day to be your best self."
— Michael Canale, *hair colorist to the stars, including Jennifer Aniston*

"This is a delightful, short, easy pool-side read! A recent widow embarks on a new journey in her retirement with surprising results! But, it isn't just a story about a retired woman's adventure, it is also a story about philanthropy!

Cynthia's writing meticulously describes the cruise ship,

the ocean views on the ship and from each villa plus the food selections of restaurant menus, in such great detail, it was as if I was physically on the cruise, seeing the stingrays or eating the food myself!

You become absorbed into the waves and marine life of the ocean in addition to the beauty of the lush tropical vegetation during the scenic trips taken on the islands. There is also an appreciation to the culture and history of the majestic Seychelle Islands. Looking forward to the next adventure in the Savannah Valley series!"

— Christina Anderson, *Retired Registered Pharmacist and Registered Nurse*

"Cynthia Manion once again proves her prowess as a storyteller with *Savannah Seas: Maiden Voyage*. Building on the wonder I felt reading *Black Pearl: A Love Letter to the Ocean*, this new voyage introduces us to the indomitable spirit of Tabitha, whose determination mirrors the very essence of the story. As readers, we are transported to the idyllic Seychelles, an island realm that Cynthia intimately knows and vividly brings to life. It's not just a tale of adventure and exploration, but also a profound narrative about setting life's compass and pursuing one's true north. Dive in and let yourself be swept away by a world of resilience, ambition, and sheer wonder."

— Joachim Buarø, *MCc Marine Technology and Aquaculture expert*

CONTENTS

PROLOGUE

Captain Charlotte Hopkins stood on deck four of Savannah Seas, the luxury cruise ship she was in charge of. She gazed down at the upturned faces of the passengers who'd soon be boarding. "Not passengers—residents," she reminded herself for the umpteenth time. The well-dressed people waiting below weren't your average cruisers, just like the Seas wasn't your average ship. It was a floating retirement community for the ultra-rich, over fifty-five crowd: some of them actual billionaires.

The idea still made Charlotte feel like she's stepped into some alternate reality. Which, come to think of it, she had.

This wasn't her first time piloting a cruise ship. She'd worked for two other luxury cruise lines since retiring from the Navy in 2009, moving up from third officer to second officer in charge of navigation, and finally, to captain five years ago. But she'd never worked on a ship like the Savannah Seas. The vessel was one of a kind, and not only because she was fitted out with wood from Brazil and tiles from India, with 3,000-plus square-foot "condos" instead of 15-square foot cabins, but also because the residents were so rich, they could afford to float from exotic port to exotic port for the rest of their lives, without a care in the world.

Charlotte, on the other hand, was responsible for the navigation, day-to-day operations, and entire crew of the ship. An awesome responsibility, but one she welcomed. She'd met with the purser, cruise director, head chef, head bartender, and ship's doctor, and they were a personable bunch, all with impressive credentials, all at the ready. She'd checked and rechecked, and the ship was ready to launch at seven p.m. Charlotte had set sail more times than she could remember, but never on a maiden voyage. She was as excited as the residents.

Glancing at her watch, she realized it was four p.m., time to meet Tabitha Leeds, the wealthiest resident onboard, and escort her to her three-bedroom condo. Mrs. Leeds had never seen it in person, only in pictures, and Charlotte hoped she liked it. (How could she not?) The captain squared her shoulders, decorated with four stripes each, smoothed the front of her dress whites, and strode down the gangplank to meet her first billionaire.

CHAPTER ONE

Failure to Launch

illionaire Tabitha Leeds stood on the red-carpeted gangway platform as she waited for a crew member to escort her on board the Savannah Seas. The luxury cruise liner was built to function as a full-service floating retirement community for those fifty-five and older, with 250 condos ranging in size from 3,000 to 6,000 square feet and priced between $2 and $10 million dollars.

Tabitha played an integral part in designing her own three-bedroom space, but today was the first time she'd be seeing it in person. All of her belongings shipped from California a week and a half before her arrival at Miami International Airport, and her two suitcases were whisked away during the check-in process a few moments ago. Despite protests from the ship's porters, she held on to her black, Louis Vuitton Bandoulière 55 weekender bag, now worn across her body so both hands remained free. It contained the basics for traveling, as well as her MacBook Air, iPad, important documents, and small, irreplaceable items she didn't feel comfortable placing in the care of anyone other than herself.

Among them was her husband's wedding ring, an

unadorned, flat sterling silver band. Five years had passed since he died, but the search for a suitable chain that would allow her to wear the ring as a necklace ornament continued. She tucked her shoulder-length, ash blond hair behind her ears and shook her head, sighing at the ridiculousness of her inability to settle for something less than perfect. Just as she was about to pull her iPhone from the back pocket of her capri jeans to check the time, she heard someone calling her name.

A blonde woman in dress whites walked down the gangway, and upon counting four stripes on her uniform, Tabitha realized it was the captain of the Savannah Seas. The woman grinned as she reached the platform, extending her right hand.

"Mrs. Leeds, I'm Captain Charlotte Hopkins. Welcome home."

Tabitha smiled as she shook the captain's hand. "Thank you, Captain Hopkins. And please, call me Tabitha."

Captain Hopkins nodded. "Will do. Feel free to call me Charlotte if you prefer."

Chuckling, Tabitha released her hand. "Someone capable of piloting such a prestigious ship deserves to be honored with a proper title, I believe. Perhaps I'll waver between the two depending on the circumstances."

"Thanks for that, Tabitha. Savannah Seas is quite the beauty, isn't she? Eleven hundred feet long, two hundred

feet at her widest point, and eighteen decks. Right up there with the rest of the world's largest cruise ships." Captain Hopkins gestured to the gangway. "We board on deck four, and your apartment is on deck fifteen. Ready to see how it turned out?"

"Yes, I am, Captain Hopkins. Lead the way."

As they boarded the ship Tabitha was awestruck by both the décor and the craftsmanship. The midship lobby, tiled with blue-galaxy quartz, boasted a ceiling of stainless steel and glass that provided a full view of the sky fourteen decks above. A welcome center was located on the right, adjacent to Savannah Strikes, the ship's bowling alley. To the left was the movie theater, Savannah Scenes, and what appeared to be a high-end clothier, Savannah Styles.

Captain Hopkins continued walking past the lobby and into a wide corridor that led to a bank of five elevators. The shade of the corridor's wool carpet mimicked that of the lobby tile, and the stainless-steel walls were accented with lighted, alternating blue and white Lucite cubes that ran along their top and bottom. Captain Hopkins pressed the up arrow of the middle elevator, and they rode in silence to the fifteenth floor. The doors opened into a long, wide hallway, but Captain Hopkins pointed to the door directly in front of them.

"Here you are, Tabitha. Apartment 1505, mid-aft, with the best possible view on any ship, in my opinion, other than being out on the top deck. It's close to the elevator, which, though convenient, might be cause for concern on other vessels, but the quality of the soundproofing on the Savannah Seas exceeds recording studio standards. You won't hear a peep, I promise. They walked you through the keyless entry process during check-in, I presume?"

Tabitha nodded. "Correct. My digital fingerprints and retina scans have been uploaded, and I downloaded the security system monitoring app as well. Have to say, I'm impressed with the level of tech I've seen so far. State-of-the-art and then some."

"Glad to hear it. It's beyond what we had on any of the ships in my fleet when I retired from the Navy two years ago." Captain Hopkins smiled, then shook her head. "Can't believe it's been that long already. Seems like it was last month."

Laughing, Tabitha shook her head as well. "I can relate. It's been three years for me, and I'm still on work time. Every day, no matter where I am or what time I went to bed, my eyes automatically open at six a.m. Will it stop at some point? Gosh, I hope so."

She paused, sizing up Captain Hopkins to determine her age. "Did I hear you say, 'your fleet?' How long were you in the Navy if you don't mind my asking?"

"I don't mind at all. Thirty years. I joined straight out of high school, worked my way up to Rear Admiral Upper

Half by the time I turned forty." Captain Hopkins smiled. "Two-star ranking. I could have gone higher, but I decided sixty percent of my base pay was more than enough to live on for the rest of my life, so I called it quits as soon as I was eligible. It was a rewarding job, but the stress was . . . well . . . a lot."

Tabitha bit her lower lip, nodding. "Those two things often go hand in hand, don't they? I loved my job. Too much, probably. It was constant pressure from my first day through my last day forty-one years later, however."

"May I ask what you did, Tabitha? I'll hazard a guess and say it involved computers or electronics since you commented on our on-board technology."

Tabitha glanced down at the floor, then back up at Captain Hopkins, smiling. "Spot on. I worked for Apple. Started back in 1977 when there was only a handful of women, but managed to stick around through all the regime changes. My role shifted from coding to product development, then to market research and public relations. I hadn't planned on retiring, but my husband was killed in South Sudan in 2016. Samuel was photographer for *National Geographic*, documenting the humanitarian crisis there. He always wanted me to travel with him to safe locations, and I always said I couldn't because of my work. I never considered that I might come to regret that choice."

She gestured to the space around them. "Doing this is my homage to his life, and I hope to understand his adventurous spirit." She sighed. "My apologies for the information dump."

Captain Hopkins reached out and patted Tabitha's shoulder. "No apologies necessary. I'm very sorry for your loss. My husband, Jacob, died in 2008. He was in the Navy as well. Our ship went down in an attack during the Iraq war. I made it, he didn't. Sometimes, we recognize that devastation in others and feel comfortable and maybe *comforted* speaking about it."

Tabitha took the captain's hand and squeezed. "I'm terribly sorry that happened to you." She smiled and Tabitha continued. "Yes, you're Charlotte now."

Charlotte chuckled. "Good. All of us on board will be spending a lot of time together, and I know soon enough we'll begin to feel like family. First-name basis is a great start." She glanced at her watch. "I'm due to meet another resident in five, so I'd best be on my way. Lovely to meet you, Tabitha. If there's anything you need, please don't hesitate to reach out."

"Thank you, Charlotte. I appreciate that."

With a wave Charlotte pushed the down arrow, stepped back into the elevator, the door shut, and she was gone. Tabitha turned her focus back to the door of apartment 1505, touching the pad of her right index finger to the

security panel to gain access to its features. Residents had the option of using the built-in retina scanner or the QR code from the Secure Savannah phone app to open their doors. She decided to test the retina version, leaning in close to allow the camera to do its work. A pleasant voice welcomed her by name, and the door opened inward. She peered around as she entered, whistling as she caught sight of the view of the Miami skyline from the twenty-foot, foldable glass veranda doors in main area.

"Wow. Home sweet home indeed."

The apartment met her specifications almost to the letter, with modifications made only to the kitchen-dining area. She'd chosen an open floor plan, but columns were added for structural support between the rooms. The flooring throughout was Brazilian macchiato pecan wood, its unique, high-contrasting tones highlighted by the soft-white painted walls. In the living room, the caramel-colored leather, Alpine-X, U-shaped sectional sofa aligned with the center of the veranda doors, facing the exterior for maximum enjoyment of the views encountered during every voyage.

The kitchen cabinets and those in all three bathrooms were constructed from the same wood as the flooring, with countertops of poured, sand-colored concrete. Two bedrooms were located toward the interior of the apartment. But the master, situated to the right of the living room, offered a seamless, floor-to-ceiling window with various levels of transparency on the outside wall. The window could be adjusted using the Savannah Security app or a bedside in-wall remote control. Though she had no plans to return to work, Tabitha had requested that the size of one guest bedroom be reduced to accommodate a fourteen-by-fourteen-foot office space in lieu of a second spare bedroom. However, she planned to monitor the time she spent sitting at her computer and step out into the real world at every opportunity.

If felt strange seeing items from her home in California here on a ship docked in Miami, but it was also somehow freeing. The moving crew had done an exceptional job placing all the furniture, so Tabitha only had to find homes for her personal items and artwork. Even her clothing was hung up, arranged in a fashion that would delight Marie Kondo. Knowing that the pantry had been stocked as well, she meandered back to the kitchen in search of a snack to tide her over until the celebration dinner an hour before sunset, after the Savannah Seas launch.

But just as she was unwrapping her fourth Lindor truffle, the ship's alarm sounded. Instinct directed her to the door, and her heart raced realizing she was locked inside. Several minutes passed before the blaring ceased, replaced by the captain's voice.

"Residents of Savannah Seas, this is Captain Hopkins speaking. Rest assured that even though we're experiencing an emergency, there is nothing wrong with the vessel. All mechanical systems are functioning normally. Your apartment doors have been locked remotely for your own protection. Federal agents have boarded the ship and are conducting a search for a fugitive who goes by the name of Brad Foster-Johnson. He's approximately six feet tall and weighs 170 pounds. We're sending a photograph of Foster-Johnson to your phones now. Please examine the image, and if you've seen this man dial 001 immediately. He is not believed to be armed but should be considered dangerous. Agents will be checking every residence. I will notify you by phone when it's your turn. Thank you for your patience and cooperation."

Tabitha sighed with relief. This was a disturbing situation, but she felt that Captain Hopkins had everything under control. And it could have been worse. Far worse. Her phone buzzed and she pulled it out of her pocket. The fugitive was blond, blue-eyed, and looked to be in his mid-thirties. She couldn't recall seeing him anywhere, either at the airport, on the docks, or at the terminal when she checked in, but the name sounded familiar.

After eating another three truffles curiosity got the better of her and she pulled her iPad out of her carry on bag and connected to the ship's Wi-Fi. The Safari browser was already open, and she typed "Brad Foster Johnson" into the Google search box. Results appeared, all showing a hyphen between "Foster" and "Johnson" and displaying the same photo she'd seen on her phone. The first headline read "Savannah Valley owner on the run, wanted for embezzlement and misappropriation of funds that bankrupted the exclusive luxury retirement community."

She touched the link with her finger to open it in a new tab. As she scanned the article, she gasped when she remembered where she saw the name before. A quick search of her gmail account located the documents she'd signed when she purchased the apartment she was currently locked inside of. Boom! There it was. Savannah Seas owner, Brad Foster-Johnson.

Tabitha set her iPad on the kitchen counter and rested her head in her hands, speaking aloud in the otherwise unoccupied space. "Oh, my lord, what if he's done the same thing with this property?" Her phone rang, scaring her half to death, and she swiped up to answer.

"Tabitha Leeds here," she said in a tremulous voice that sounded higher than normal.

"Tabitha, it's Captain Hopkins. Charlotte. How are you holding up?"

"Um . . . well . . . I've been better. I decided to Google and—"

"I did as well. Let's put that aside for the moment.

I'm outside your door now with two agents. I'm going to unlock it if that's all right with you. Are you alone?"

Though no one could see, Tabitha nodded. "Yes. Just me in here alone with my thoughts. Should I stay in a particular spot?"

"That's a great idea. Where will you be?"

Tabitha unwrapped another truffle and popped it into her mouth. "At the kitchen counter binging on candy."

Charlotte chuckled. "Sounds like a good plan to me." She paused, and Tabitha heard the door unlock. "Okay, we're coming in. Agents first, Bob Matalin followed by Rick Sterns. Then me."

Two men dressed in dark suits and ties entered the room and nodded to Tabitha. "Do we have your permission to search the apartment, ma'am?" the agent called Bob asked. When Tabitha nodded, Bob and Rick headed in opposite directions.

"I can't put this aside, Charlotte. Did you see what I saw? That the man they're looking for is the owner of Savannah Seas? And that he bankrupted another retirement community he owned? What if he did the same thing with this property?"

Charlotte nodded. "Yes, I did. Since we hadn't set sail yet, all the accounting was done off-site. The on-board guy was supposed to be here this morning, but he never showed up. Turns out he was the executive director at Savannah

Valley, Devan Strong. They arrested him a week ago and he's being held without bail."

Tabitha exhaled and shook her head again. "Well, that's not good news. What's going to happen here, do you think?"

Charlotte shrugged. "I have no clue what the future holds, but there's one thing I do know with certainty. Savannah Seas won't be launching, at least not today."

CHAPTER TWO

Saving a Sinking Ship

Three days later, Tabitha sat at the Captain's table in the Savannah Seas main dining room. It was an exact replica of the first-class dining room of the Queen Mary, including a digital version of the famous map of the ship's route between Europe and the Americas. At the moment, a Zoom meeting was on the screen, with the faces of many part-time Savannah Seas residents on display in gallery view. When Derek Donahue took his place in the center of the room, the conversations between the full-time residents seated at the tables around him ceased.

"Hello, all. Thanks for coming," he said. "I've met all of you in the room, but for those attending virtually, I'm Derek Donahue, Savannah Seas purser. We're discussing major issues today that involve big money, and I want you to know that as the former manager of the Bellagio Hotel and Casino in Las Vegas, I have significant experience in dealing with such matters." He grinned, blue eyes twinkling in the glow of the ring light. "So much for retiring from that kind of work."

The sound of laughter resonated in the open space as Derek continued. "Ah, your sense of humor is still intact.

Good. I know for me, when that goes, it means stuff has really hit the fan." He sobered. "The past few days have been challenging, and I thank you for your patience as we evaluated our situation and attempted to find a path forward. Captain Hopkins, Tabitha Leeds, Elaine Greer, and I believe we've done so, and we'd like to propose our solution to you now. Tabitha, will you join me please?"

Tabitha rose from her chair, then walked to the center of the room. Derek passed her a microphone. She swallowed, took a deep breath, then spoke. "Hi everyone. Good to see you again, and nice to meet those of you who've yet to join us aboard. My name is Tabitha Leeds. I'm a California girl, spent my entire career at Apple, and retired in 2018. There weren't many opportunities for me to travel while I was working, so I decided spending my retirement on a never-ending cruise sounded like a great way to make up for lost time. Not off to a good start in that department, am I?"

A few chuckles emanated from the crowd, and Tabitha went on. "I'm sure many of you have Googled Mr. Foster-Johnson over the past three days, and if you did, you know that he embezzled funds from and bankrupted Savannah Valley, a community like ours but on land. The FBI informed Captain Hopkins this morning that they found Mr. Foster-Johnson yesterday hiding off the coast of the Florida Keys on a yacht he'd purchased with stolen funds.

He's being held without bail, so we don't have to worry about him showing up anytime soon, but we do have to worry about cleaning up the mess he left behind. I reached out to Savannah Valley with the hope that we'd be able to help each other find solutions since our financial situations are similar. As it turned out, they already had one. Captain Hopkins, Derek, Elaine, and I ran all the numbers, and their solution will work for us as well, if you're all willing to give it a go."

Murmurs and whispers broke the silence of both the physical and virtual rooms. Tabitha waited for things to quiet down before continuing. She smiled as she held her left hand out, palm up. "Several residents of Savannah Valley combined their financial resources and purchased the community outright. The monthly dues will cover all the community's expenses, and they'll begin to show a profit within the next two years."

Loud gasps and a few expletives were replaced with excited chatter within the space of two minutes. Tabitha paused until it dissipated. "Well, it sounds like most of you are indeed willing, and you haven't even heard the details yet." She turned to Derek. "Will you pull those up and share your screen, please?" He nodded, and when the information was visible on the large screen, Tabitha waved Elaine over.

"Folks, this is Elaine Greer. While she isn't an

accountant, she did manage the finances for her ex-husband's business. He's an investment banker, and she walked away with a $1.5 billion-dollar divorce settlement, so I trust her judgment."

Elaine navigated from her table to the middle of the room, her waist-length brown braid swinging. She laughed as she took the mic. Tabitha grinned and took three steps backward, allowing the other woman to take the floor. "Well, I have to say, that's now my favorite introduction."

Nodding, Elaine pointed at the screen. "Let's all look at the information Tabitha, Derek, Captain Hopkins, and I compiled. The total cost to build and furnish the Savannah Seas was just over $1.5 billion dollars. The amount we paid for our apartments covered that cost and then some, but Mr. Foster-Johnson borrowed against the ship's value. As of today, there's an outstanding lien in place for almost $2 billion dollars. If it's not paid, the lienholder can take possession of the Savannah Seas and we'll lose everything."

Elaine paused in anticipation of comments, but there were none. "Derek, next slide please. On this screen is what we're proposing to prevent that from happening. Option one, every resident contributes the exact amount of funds they paid for their apartment and becomes an invested cooperative owner of the Savannah Seas. Option two, a limited number of residents contribute larger sums and become co-owners of the Savannah Seas by forming a limited liability corporation. With either option, all residents will pay the monthly dues amount agreed to in their original purchase contract. The collected dues will be used to pay for all expenses, including fuel, the crew's salaries, food, and entertainment. By my math, there's plenty left over for maintenance and repairs that will be needed down the line." She turned to glance at Tabitha. "Back to you, Tabitha. A lame segue, I know, but it'll have to do."

Tabitha chuckled as she stepped forward to retrieve the microphone from Elaine. "It makes me feel like a field reporter. I'll take it." She looked around the room. "That was a lot to absorb, I know. None of us expected to be in this situation, faced with losing our homes, be it part-time or full. We're supposed to be on our way to the Seychelles Islands, enjoying ourselves and getting to know each other. Swimming in the open ocean air. Laying out on the decks in the sun. Eating delicious meals. Waking up each morning with the day's events unplanned, our schedules wide open. Wealthy nomads relaxing in luxury on a continuous journey around the world."

Tabitha thought about how Samuel had spent so many years travelling under conditions that were the opposite of what she'd just described. If this ship didn't sail, it would feel like she'd lost him all over again. Squaring her shoulders, Tabitha continued, "We dream of these things all our lives, the things we'll do when we retire. How we'll spend our golden years. We worked hard to reach this moment, we lived to see this moment, and we deserve to have our dreams become a reality. No stranger should be able to steal that from us, should they? No. They shouldn't. And I'll tell you right now that the Savannah Seas will launch, even if I need to pay off the entire lien myself."

The audience—both in-person and virtual—exploded in applause. Tabitha blinked, stunned by the positive reaction to her statements. Derek returned to her side, and she passed him the microphone when he held out his hand. He smiled at her, then gave her a thumbs up.

Once the noise died down, Derek tapped the microphone three times and then spoke. "That applause was well deserved. Thank you, Tabitha. Excellent points, and anyone left uninspired by the last bit should check themselves for a pulse." Laughter rang out as he continued. "There's a great deal at stake for every member of our staff and crew, and for me as well. Please know that we all appreciate your willingness to consider moving forward and keeping the Savannah Seas operational more than words can say, and we hope we have the opportunity to express our gratitude with our actions as we create and curate the experiences that will make your dreams come true."

More applause ensued and was interrupted by Captain

Hopkins taking the floor. She spoke sans microphone. "Hello there. Can everyone hear me?" A chorus of yeses answered her query. "Great, thank you. Please don't feel pressured to decide right now if you'll be buying in, but we will need a firm yes or no within the next forty-eight hours. I've sent out an email to all of you with a contract attached. Please reply and indicate your intention. If you respond in the affirmative, return your contract before the forty-eight hours elapse. Those who choose to become part owners of Savannah Seas will meet here three days from now, Wednesday, at noon. Derek, Elaine, Tabitha, and I will remain here for another hour or two to answer any questions you may have, and feel free to reach out via email, text, or phone at any time. My door is always open. Have a wonderful rest of the day!"

Captain Hopkins's phone chimed before she had a chance to join the others at the table they chose as their interim office. The residents began to queue up to talk to Elaine, Tabitha, and Derek or were chatting in small, excited groups. The captain entered her PIN and opened her email to find that one hundred responses had come in, all of them a yes. The chiming continued as she made her way through the crowd to the others.

Tabitha waved and shouted over the din. "Do you have any contracts? They want contracts. They don't want to wait. They want to sign right now."

Four hours later, Tabitha, Derek, Elaine, and Charlotte were still in the dining room. All but five of the 250 residents had opted in, and 245 contracts were signed. The five waiting to opt in were seeking advice from their attorneys before proceeding but had every intention of participating.

Elaine leaned back in her chair, smiling as she shook her head. "That was such a great speech, Tabitha. Talk about a positive response."

"Looks like all my public relations experience finally paid off," Tabitha said. Then she frowned, disappointed in herself for deflecting instead of accepting the compliment. She smiled and reversed course. "Thank you, Elaine. I'm glad you thought it was great. It was from the heart, and knowing it was well received makes me feel good about putting myself out there."

Elaine reached out and patted Tabitha's hand. "You putting yourself out there was the catalyst for saving a sinking ship. Great work."

Charlotte nodded. "Really great work. You rallied your fellow nomads. Be proud."

Derek leaned forward, resting his elbows on the table. "So, you were serious about paying off the lien yourself?"

"One hundred percent, Derek," Tabitha nodded.

Derek stared down at the table for several seconds before responding. He shook his head. "I'm sorry, I hope I didn't offend you. Working in Vegas . . . well . . . it was cutthroat. Eat or be eaten. The higher ups had more money than they could ever spend in a lifetime but expected employees to live on next to nothing. More work, less pay was the corporate motto. They'd lay someone off, give them a $1,000 casino credit as a parting gift, then go after them when they fell into debt. Toward the end of my stint as manager, I found myself deeming such behavior acceptable because everything was about the bottom line. That's when I knew it was time to go. Genuine generosity in any form was nowhere to be found in my life, so I suppose I'd forgotten it was possible. Again, my apologies."

Tabitha shook her head. "No need to apologize, Derek. I understand. There was financial generosity for employees where I was, but we went through some long stretches of emotional bankruptcy. I've never related to the concept of hoarding wealth. Seriously—I'm sitting on $3 billion dollars, I don't have children and I'm seventy. That's a $100 million a year to spend if I live to see 100. I can't take it with me when I die, so why not do something useful with it while I'm alive?" She sighed. "I must be honest, though. In this instance my initial motivation was pure selfishness. I wasn't thinking of anyone other than myself and my late husband. This whole undertaking is to honor him and the life he chose to live. A selfless life. He risked everything to show the truth of the world to others while I sat safe in my office. I can't let him down. Not again."

Charlotte wrapped her arm around Tabitha's shoulders. "Don't be so hard on yourself, Tabitha. We're all doing the best we can with what we have. Perhaps your motivation was selfish, but your words inspired a great deal of generosity in others, and that's amazing."

Elaine nodded. "That's right, Charlotte. It is amazing. I think Samuel would be pleased that your insistence in honoring his memory served to foster goodness in some and provide financial security for others."

Tabitha looked at her companions in turn. "Thanks, all. Yes, you're right, Elaine. He would be pleased. And don't get me wrong—I enjoy the freedoms my financial status allows me. I know that I'm a privileged person. Because I had it all, as the saying goes, I never stopped to consider that there might be more to life until Samuel died. I'm blessed to have the opportunity to explore that theory, and that exploration begins with this ship launching. Let's get back to business, shall we? Our first adventure together awaits. Seychelles, here we come!"

CHAPTER THREE

Sharing Their Stories

he participation of all full- and part-time residents of the Savannah Seas was confirmed at the start of the noon meeting on Wednesday. When it came to making decisions, each person would have one vote regardless of the amount of their financial outlay. But the group thought it best to establish a board of directors to handle the oversight of day-to-day business, including the ship's management-level staff. Tabitha, Elaine, and two other full-time residents, Doris Collins and Lorenzo Ricci, were nominated and approved for the roles of president, treasurer, secretary, and vice president, respectively. The meeting ended a half-hour later for the residents, but the board remained to confer with Savannah Seas management to go over the basics of how the ship operated.

Tabitha's phone dinged, and she picked it up off the table to see who was texting her. She read the message, then put her phone down and turned her attention to her fellow board members. "That was Captain Hopkins. She and the others will be here in ten minutes."

Lorenzo smiled. "Good. That gives us a little time to get to know each other better. I'll start. So, you know from what my friend Maria said when she nominated me that I was Olive Garden's franchise and expansion manager for thirty years. Let me tell you how I ended up there. My parents were first generation Italian immigrants, and they opened Italia Ricci in Brooklyn in 1950. I started managing the place when I was still in high school, and by 1984 we had twenty-five locations across all five boroughs. The Olive Garden corporate guys ate at every one of them, then came to see me. They offered me the job on the spot, and I went for it. Most of the Italia Riccis became Olive Gardens, and some went under, but the original is still up and running. My wife, Serena, took it over for me in 1986, but my boys, Joey and Leonardo, own it now. Serena passed in 2017, the year after I retired. Breast cancer."

Lorenzo closed his eyes as he ran his right hand through his silver hair. "I'm here because Brooklyn just isn't the same without her, and I don't think I'll ever be able to call someplace else home. I figure this way I don't have to, you know?"

Doris shook her head, her dark, high-teased hair unmoving. "Lorenzo, I understand," she said in her melodic southern accent. "My Buck passed in 2020 after a six-year go-round with lung cancer. Beauregard Collins, CFO of Texas Instruments since 1982. He had to stop working in 2015. Didn't want to, but the chemo took too much out of him. We had a wonderful life together. House in Shadow Lawn, Texas. That's the museum district. I got to be a stay-at-home mom, and we had full-time kitchen and housekeeping help. That allowed me to spend a great deal of time with the children, three girls and two boys. They're why I'm here. When Buck passed, the children encouraged me to go out and explore the world. They said it was something I hadn't done because I was too busy raising them." She smiled. "I guess I did a decent job of it."

Elaine nodded. "Yes, you did. Thanks for sharing your story, and Lorenzo, thanks for sharing yours. You know mine already. Tabitha, would you like to share yours?"

"Sure. I'll make it brief in case the others arrive sooner than expected." Tabitha took a deep breath. "I went to work for Apple in 1977 and retired in 2018. My husband, Samuel, was a photographer for *National Geographic*. He was killed on a shoot in South Sudan in 2016. I didn't take the time to travel with him because I was so involved in my work, which I regret. Being aboard the Savannah Seas is my homage to his life."

Nodding, Lorenzo reached across the table and placed his hand on top of Tabitha's. "That is a lovely sentiment. We should all be so fortunate to have someone honor our memory in such a way after we pass on."

As Tabitha was about to thank him, Captain Hopkins entered the room with five people in tow. She introduced them, pointing to each in turn as she spoke. "You've already met our purser, Derek Donahue. This is Quinton Mays, cruise director; Ollie Shivley, head chef; Ilse Blue, head bartender; and Caroline Peterman, ship physician."

All six took a seat at the table with the board. "What department would you like us to begin with?"

Tabitha glanced at the other board members, each of them shrugging as her eyes met theirs. "I guess it's up to you. I don't think any of us have experience with the operational aspects of a cruise ship."

Doris raised her hand. "Does being a huge fan of the *Love Boat* count?"

Everyone laughed and Captain Hopkins nodded. "You know what? It does count. You know all the basics of the staff hierarchy. There's one role that wasn't accurately portrayed in the show, though, so let's start there. Derek, you're up."

Derek chuckled. "No shade to Gopher, but the purser isn't just a luggage boy. The title of the position is indicative of what the work entails: purser, purse. What's in a purse? Historically, money. I function as the head of accounting and customer service, and I'm also responsible for handing immigration, travel documents, and customs issues. Desk, concierge, and housekeeping staff work under my authority. Kicking the football to you, Ollie."

"Some folks call me Ollie, others call me Shiv, and on occasion I'm called names that I won't repeat in present company." Ollie chuckled and the other staff members joined in. "As Head Chef, I'm in charge of the kitchen, pantry, and food delivery staff. It's my job to ensure that you receive the most delicious food and impeccable service that money can buy at every meal. I'm thirty-five and spent the past four years working as a sous-chef under Gordon Ramsay."

Elaine's brows rose. "And you survived? That's all I need to know, Ollie."

Ollie threw back his head and laughed. "Yeah, he spewed some insults I won't repeat. But in all honesty, it was the best experience of my career so far. I learned more in those four years than most chefs do in twenty. I wanted to travel though, and as soon as I saw the Savannah Seas listing I thought, *this is it*. I'm very grateful to be here."

He nodded toward Derek. "Derek and I work together as a team for the most part, and he's integral to our being able to maintain our stock as we travel around the world. Every port has different customs regulations for food and beverage, and I provide him with a list of everything we need well in advance to make sure nothing goes awry. Don't want you to end up eating peanut butter and jelly! Not that there's anything wrong with that, so if anyone wants a PB&J, I'll whip it together. Crusts off, even." Everyone chuckled and Ollie grinned.

Quinton waved to everyone at the table. "Hello, all.

I'm the Savannah Seas cruise director. Prior to this grand adventure I was the creative and senior show director at Disney World. Fun is in my blood, and that's my singular goal—all of you having the best time ever, no matter what you're doing. My departments are hospitality, entertainment, and activities, the latter both on board and off. Once we launch, my voice will be the one you hear over the loudspeaker morning, noon, and night. I'll always be lurking in the shadows, waiting for the moment when a resident is no longer smiling so I can leap out into the light and turn that frown upside down."

Quinton grinned, using his index fingers to turn up the corners of his mouth. "But seriously, I'm here to serve our residents in any capacity that helps them live their best lives. Mental wellness can be difficult to maintain as we age, especially when we experience loss or trauma. Exercise, entertainment, and social interaction are the keys to keeping ourselves mentally healthy, and I carefully consider those components when I'm planning events and activities." He paused. "Hmm, I'm not sure if I should pass this along to our head bartender or our doctor."

Doctor Peterman snorted. "We both serve as therapists from time to time. I'll take my turn now if it's okay with you, Ilse. I'm Caroline Peterman, recently retired director of operations for Universal Health Services. I served in that position for fifteen years, during which I became

increasingly detached from what drove me to become a doctor . . . caring for patients. I resigned on my sixty-second birthday with the intention of travelling for a year or two to reorient my moral compass.

"While researching cruises, I came across Savannah Seas and decided to purchase an apartment. By mistake, I navigated to the career opportunities page instead of the application and saw that the position of ship physician was open. Two birds, one stone as they say. I'm thrilled, both to be returning to my roots, and seeing the world. As you'd expect, everything medical related falls under my umbrella. We have a team of surgeons, nurses, anesthetists, and rehabilitation specialists, as well as a fully stocked pharmacy, and the most innovative and technologically advanced equipment available at the ready. Connections with all planned destinations have been made, and our on-board helicopter functions as a medical transport, if needed. No problem is too small—I even treat hangovers."

Ilse chuckled. "Speaking of hangovers—I'm how you manage to get one. My official title is Savannah Seas head bartender, though I prefer the term 'mixologist.' I'm thirty-seven, and my most recent position was as assistant manager under Tom Walker at the Fontainebleau Hotel in Miami. Long story short, I felt it was time for me to move on from being someone's assistant and stand on my own.

On this ship, it's my job to procure the supplies to

create any mixed drink a resident is in the mood for, as well as stock preferred wines and beers as per the list provided with resident contracts. So, if Mr. Ricci finishes off a bottle of 2004 Penfolds Block 42 Cabernet Sauvignon and I don't have a another waiting for him, I've failed. I don't like to fail, so I typically move heaven and earth to avoid a mistake before it happens, like slipping away in one of our small boats to meet a courier in the middle of the night on shore. Which I instantly regret mentioning because now if you see dark circles under my eyes, you'll know I've screwed something up."

Everyone laughed and Ilse continued. "I enjoy creating new mixes, so I'll be encouraging our residents to submit suggestions. Maybe at some point one will take off and be served in fine establishments all over the planet. Or not so fine establishments. Either works for me. But both would be better."

Captain Hopkins tapped the tabletop with both hands. "And there you have it. I suggest that the board take some time to tour areas of the ship that are normally off limits to residents, like the galleys, pantries, staff quarters, and the engine room. It's helpful to know the ins and outs of the way things operate before problems arise. Not that I anticipate issues other than those we need to resolve so we can launch. But those are all off-board. I'm now going to conduct a regular crew-leaders meeting, if that's okay

with the rest of you." Tabitha, Elaine, Doris, and Lorenzo nodded. "Great. Derek, where do we stand financially and with our routing?"

Derek opened his Chromebook. "We need to pay off the lien in full and transfer ownership of the Savannah Seas before we can leave the dock. All owner payments are in process and should post tomorrow or Friday at the latest. When they do, I'll wire the funds to the lienholder via instant transfer. They've promised to provide proof of ownership upon receipt of payment. I hope to have all sale-related tasks taken care of by the close of business Friday, at which point I can solidify our route and docking in the Seychelles. Things are in play for launching any day next week; I just need to notify all involved parties twenty-four hours in advance. Customs paperwork just needs to be dated, signed, and submitted."

"Nice job, Derek. Thank you." Captain Hopkins turned to Ollie. "What's the status of provisions, Ollie?"

"All our destination suppliers have held our non-perishables for us, and perishables on that end are readily available with twelve hours' notice. I've tracked what's been used here in port and will place our orders as soon as launch is confirmed. The cut off for a same-day order is five a.m., so I need to know when we're launching by midnight the night before at the latest."

"Excellent. We'll make sure you have more notice than that, Ollie. How about you, Ilse?"

"Same as Shiv. I mean Ollie. I'll save Shiv for private conversations, so I don't confuse the heck out of everyone. The only exceptions would be rarer commodities that might need to be aired in from somewhere, so it's best if I know twenty-four hours in advance at minimum."

Captain Hopkins nodded. "Duly noted. Thank you for staying on top of things, Ilse. Doctor Peterman, anything needed in your department?"

"We're in great shape," the doctor said. "I've checked a lot of blood pressures and handed out a few bottles of ibuprofen and acetaminophen, but other than that, nada. I did modify resident prescription orders scheduled to be delivered when we dock in the Seychelles to include an extra month for everything. Better to err on the side of caution."

"Very true." Captain Hopkins pulled her phone from her pocket, swiping on the screen as she spoke. "Engineering will test all systems daily as per usual and conduct an emergency evacuation drill one day before launch. Fuel will be delivered then. I think I'll schedule two more launch procedure practices, as well. Quinton, is there anything you need to address?"

"No ma'am. I'm all set for the duration of our journey, and my contacts in the Seychelles are on standby. I'll notify them of our launch date, and they can reconfigure our itinerary based on our anticipated arrival time. If all else fails, I can always break out the balloon animals."

Captain Hopkins rolled her eyes, then laughed. "I'm going to hold you to that, Quinton. Even though I harbor an intense dislike for balloons in general. So many bad sounds." Quinton stood as she pointed at him with her left index finger. "Don't even think about it, Quinton. Sit your butt back down on that chair right now."

Quinton grinned. "Captain's orders?"

"Yes. Captain's orders." Charlotte shuddered. "Ugh, now you all know my singular, irrational fear."

Quinton opened his mouth to speak but was cut off by the captain before he was able to utter a word.

"Quinton Mays, if you say you'll try not to hold it against me and then make a squeaky balloon noise, I'll fire you. For real."

Raucous laughter ensued, and as it faded, Tabitha sat in awe of all she'd heard. "Wow, thank you for allowing us to be a part of this," she said. "The level of precision that's required to keep our floating home operating is astonishing. It's not something people think about when they're on vacation, all the effort that's expended behind the scenes. It's structured so they don't notice, I suppose. Fascinating." She paused, then stood, raising an imaginary glass. "To all of you, and the rest of the crew. You make the impossible possible, and I salute you."

Her words were echoed by Elaine, Doris, and Lorenzo, and Captain Hopkins blushed at the attention. The staff returned to work, and Tabitha went back to her cabin to change into her bathing suit. The Miami sun was strong, and basking in it seemed like a perfect way to celebrate the huge leap forward toward the ship's launch. She smiled as she unbuttoned her polo shirt and thought, "Not *the* ship. *Our* ship. In part, *my* ship. I bought a ship! Weird, wild stuff."

CHAPTER FOUR

Smooth Sailing

"As your captain, I hereby christen this vessel the Savannah Seas." Captain Hopkins smashed the bottle of 1996 Dom Perignon Rose Gold Methuselah against the prow railing. Cheers and whoops erupted from the ship's full-time residents, as well as the part-timers attending virtually via Zoom.

Tabitha raised her glass of champagne high in the air and shouted, "To the Savannah Seas!" All the residents echoed her sentiment. They began to disperse as the staff rolled up the red carpet where the captain had been standing. Launch was scheduled to begin in fifteen minutes, and Derek waved everyone to the fifty-foot-long portion of railing he decorated for the occasion.

"Come on down, all!" he called. We're going to have ourselves a little maiden voyage send-off party out here before the big bash inside later. We didn't give you a proper lei you when you arrived, so we're going to do it now. There's a haku lei waiting for you, too. Line up, please. Single file."

Tropical music played from a small set of wireless speakers, and servers arrived with trays of glasses filled with milky-white liquid. "Surrender your champagne to the servers, and indulge in your first taste of the Seychelles— palm wine. The traditional drink of the locals, who call it 'kalou,' and it's made from, you guessed it, palm trees. The sap of palm trees, to be precise. It's gathered like maple syrup, left to sit, and two hours later has a four percent alcohol content. It's naturally sweet, but the longer it ferments the more sour and bitter it becomes. Much like me." He grinned. "Kidding, kidding. Probably. What we have for you leans sweet and goes down easy, so drink responsibly. More than two of those, and you won't only miss tonight's celebration, you might be out of commission until we arrive in the Seychelles."

Tabitha, midway back in the line, removed a glass of palm wine from the server's tray and replaced it with what was left of her champagne. She took a small sip, closed her eyes, and let her body sway to the music as she imagined what it was going to feel like to sitting on a beach and listening to the sound of the waves as they rolled in and out. A tap on the shoulder pulled her from her daydream. She spun around to see who the culprit was.

Elaine smiled. "Sorry, I didn't mean to frighten you. Irene and her husband, Russ, were in front of me, but they wanted to use the restrooms now so they wouldn't miss us leaving the dock. Lost in your thoughts?"

Tabitha nodded as she moved forward six steps to catch up to the rest of the line. "Fantasizing about hanging out on the beach and listening to the water." She held up her drink. "Preferably with one of these in my hand. Only one sip so far and I'm hooked."

Elaine raised her glass and clinked it with Tabitha's. "Yet another cheer. To enjoying what's to come."

Grinning, Tabitha took another sip of her palm wine. "To enjoying what's to come. Especially if it's another one of these."

The wait to reach Derek was less than two minutes. Both women received their tropicbird orchid and palm frond leis as well as pink frangipani flower crowns, then joined the other residents at the railing. Captain Hopkins's voice rang out over the PA system.

"Attention Savannah Seas residents. Launch begins in five, four, three, two, one. Ladies and gentlemen, we're off! Please enjoy the view as we leave port and enter open waters. I look forward to seeing you at our maiden voyage celebration this evening. Please stop by the captain's table to say hello to your crew leaders and board of directors."

Elaine elbowed Tabitha. "Guess we're eating at the captain's table, eh?"

Tabitha shrugged. "I guess so. In which case, I'm going to head back to my apartment now because the blue collared blouse and white linen capri pants I picked out no longer seem appropriate, and all my dresses are still bagged. I have no clue what's what."

Chuckling, Elaine pointed at Tabitha. "Why not just close your eyes, put your hand out, and go with the first dress you touch?"

"As much as I'd like to, my wedding dress is among them and with my luck . . ."

"Well now I wish I'd saved mine. Imagine the looks we'd get. I do have a black silk pantsuit I could wear, though."

Snorting, Tabitha gave Elaine's shoulder a playful nudge. "Listen, my wedding dressed is so stained and musty, if someone said 'Beetlejuice' three times, we'd have a real bash on our hands."

Tabitha stood in the ladies lounge just outside the main dining room, turning from side to side as she evaluated her reflection in the full-length mirror. She'd chosen a black, tea-length silk and crepe Valentino San Gallo Edition dress from the second garment bag she unzipped. The dress always served her well at corporate parties, as had the matte-black Kate Louboutins. Around her neck she wore a diamond web necklace by Paul Morelli, the last birthday gift she received from Samuel. It glittered in the warm LED light, and she smiled as she recalled how thrilled he was that he managed to surprise her. She wore her hair wound up in a bun, wisps that escaped on the journey downstairs curled at her temples and the base of her neck. She rolled

her eyes and pulled at one of the curls, then let it go and felt it bounce back.

"Well, I should have taken the elevator. Humidity is no friend to this hair," Tabitha said aloud. She exited the bathroom, turned left, then left again into the main dining room. Fairy lights were strung above the buffet tables in the center of the room, and all the tables were covered in gold and white cloths. When she reached the captain's table, she realized that what she thought was a printed pattern was actually a hand-painted, abstract design in iridescent white, yellow, and purple. Captain Hopkins rose from her chair, as did the crew leaders, Lorenzo and Elaine.

"Good evening, Tabitha. Please sit down. Doris texted me to say she'll be a few minutes late and would like us to proceed without her."

Everyone sat, and Captain Hopkins signaled the cocktail waiter. The table decided to share a bottle of Pomerol Petrus circa 2016, grown, crafted, and aged in France's Bordeaux region. As they finished their first glass, Doris arrived, clad in a canary yellow, sleeveless ball gown. Elaine whistled.

"Wow, Doris. That's gorgeous. It's the perfect color for you."

Doris curtsied. "Why, thank you very much. It's Oscar de la Renta, my favorite designer. I love a sweetheart neckline. Makes my hair look bigger." She patted her updo.

"You know what they say in Texas: the higher the hair, the closer to God." Everyone at the table laughed. "I'm terribly sorry for my lateness. I believe I saw Iberian ham being sliced on the buffet line and cannot wait to see what other delicacies await us."

Lorenzo rose to pull out Doris's chair but was interrupted by Captain Hopkins. "Now that we're all here, let's dig in, shall we?" The others nodded, and Hopkins navigated her way to the buffet's starting point, waving to indicate that they should follow her. In addition to the Iberian ham, more than fifty options awaited them, including Wagyu beef sliders, seared matsutake mushrooms, Keluga supreme caviar served on saffron crackers, black Ayam Cemani chicken and Swedish moose cheese skewers, Japan tuna sushi, and Bonnotte potatoes stuffed with Kurobuta bacon and Pule donkey cheese.

The group was quiet as they ate, other than an occasional comment on how fabulous a particular food item tasted. Forty-five minutes passed before the return trips to the buffet ceased, and soon after the servers cleared the remaining plates from the table. A team arrived to break down the buffet and wheel the stations away to make room for dancing. Captain Hopkins excused herself to go out onto the floor and address the residents. Derek followed, grabbed a microphone from the sound and stage staff who were setting up the DJ booth, then handed it off to Captain Hopkins before returning to his seat.

She smiled, her dress whites bright and pressed to perfection. "I hope you all enjoyed your dinner." Thunderous applause echoed throughout the room. She laughed. "I'll take that as a yes. As you can see, we're getting things ready for the after-dinner dance party, and while you wait, dessert will be served. I hope you aren't disappointed because there's only one option."

She paused as a giant replica of the Savannah Seas was rolled into the room. "Cake! Created for us by Debbie Wingham, one of the world's top ten cake artists and flown in last night from England. It weighs just under 500 pounds, and it's sized to scale down to the last detail. Take your photos now because Chef Shivley's crew will be cutting it up in just a few minutes."

Captain Hopkins returned to the table, beaming. "They sent a sample tasting cake along with it, and I can personally assure you it's the most delicious thing I've had in my entire life. Layers of vanilla bean and Belgian chocolate cake layers with alternating mascarpone and chocolate truffle cream. One of Debbie's other cakes sold for $75 million, and I understand why. This took 400 hours to create."

When the server delivered slices to their table, Tabitha stared at her plate, shaking her head. "Nothing can be that good, can it?"

Doris was already on her third forkful. "Yes, honey. Yes, it can. Give it a go and you'll see."

Tabitha made sure she had a bit of everything on her fork, both layer types and creams. When it hit her taste buds, the flavor elicited a moan of pleasure. "My god, it really can. Holy moly mother of pearl. I wasn't planning on dancing, but this makes me want to get up and get down like never before. Derek, what type of music will the DJ be playing?"

"Whatever you wish, Tabitha. He's got some celebration favorites lined up, but other than that the playlist is wide open. What did you have in mind?" He winked at her. "I may have enough pull to get your request to the top of the roster."

Tabitha stroked her chin. "Hmm, I think some Harry Belafonte is in order, maybe *Jump in the Line*? And some disco—oh, I have the perfect song. The Bee Gees, *Stayin' Alive*."

Elaine shrieked. "Oh my god, yes, that's perfect. How about Gloria Gaynor's *I Will Survive*?"

Doris placed her fork across her empty plate, tines down. "There are lots of widows 'round these parts, so we simply must hear *It's Raining Men* by the Weather Girls."

Captain Hopkins laughed so hard that she was unable to catch her breath for several moments. When she composed herself enough to speak, she managed to blurt out "*Single Ladies* by Beyoncé," before the laughter resumed with the entire table joining in.

True to his word, Derek had their requests bumped to the top of the queue. As the first strains of *Stayin' Alive* began to play, Tabitha and Elaine ran out onto the dance floor in their bare feet, heels left under the table. Only a few residents remained on the sidelines, and Tabitha pulled on Elaine's sleeve, shouting above the music.

"I'm surprised that so many people are dancing. Usually, it's the other way around."

Elaine nodded. "Me too. I'm glad, though. Must be a fun bunch we're living with here."

Doris shimmied over to them. "It *is* a fun bunch. I've already made two new friends. I think that it has something to do with being of a certain age, too."

"What do you mean?" Doris shook her head and Tabitha cupped her hands to her mouth and shouted, "I said what do you mean?"

Doris leaned in. "I mean when we reach a certain age our inhibitions fly out the window. Our time is short, so we do what we want, and we don't care a whit who's watching or what they think about us."

The song ended as Tabitha nodded. "Doris, I believe you have a valid point there. I cut loose here and there throughout my life, but me thirty years ago would never have been the first one out on the dance floor, especially in front of people I hadn't even met." She grinned. "But look at me now. Introduce me to your new friends, won't you,

Doris? I'm making tonight's goal to meet as many fellow residents as possible. Hmm, we should have nametags." As *I Will Survive* began playing, she spotted Derek across the room and waved him over.

"What can I do you for, my dearest Tabitha? More song requests?"

Tabitha shook her head. "No. Well, not yet. We were wondering if you happened to have any nametags. We're going to introduce ourselves to as many residents as possible tonight, and it would be easier for others to do the same if we had nametags, don't you think?"

Derek put his hand on his hip. "What a fantastic idea." He leaned forward, peering into Tabitha's eyes. "You're not trying to steal my job, are you?"

Tabitha chuckled. "Nope. No way. I'm done with jobs." Derek nodded. "Okay then. I'll go grab those nametags.

Be right back." He jogged off, returning before the song ended, out of breath when he spoke. "Lucky for me they had some in the galley. I thought I remembered them wearing stickers while Ollie had their permanent nametags made. Let's all take a pile and a pen and work the room, gals."

One hour and two repeats of *It's Raining Men* later, every resident had a nametag stuck on their designer clothing. Tabitha interacted with everyone, even if it was just a simple "hello" and the presentation of a tag. *Single*

Ladies, which was bumped by other requests began to play, and not a single resident remained seated. Crew members were pulled onto the dance floor from the sidelines.

Tabitha looked around the room as she turned in a circle with her hands in the air. She saw new faces that would grow familiar, acquaintances that might become friends. All strangers until boarding the Savannah Seas. This had been Samuel's life, traveling the world and meeting new people. For the first time, a door into his world opened, and she felt pure joy at the prospect of someday walking right through it.

CHAPTER FIVE

Seeing Seychelles
Mahé

Tabitha stood at the railing of the Savannah Seas deck four railing while she waited to disembark.

The ship was scheduled to dock at the Victoria port at sunrise, and after all the residents got safely ashore, Captain Hopkins would sail it back out into the Indian Ocean. There, just off the coast, the Savannah Seas would remain moored for four days. Two weeks was allotted for the maiden voyage as the residents explored three of the 115 islands that comprised the Seychelles' archipelago, located just north of Madagascar. Many residents booked hotels or villas on Mahé, the first island of their itinerary, but some chose to travel back and forth from Mahé to the Savannah Seas using the ship's tender, so they could sleep in their own apartments.

Tabitha, Elaine, and Doris each reserved their own beachside room at Anantara Maia Seychelles Villas, which offered round-the-clock concierge service, guided walking tours, an aerial tour of the island via helicopter, yoga, massages, and more. Except for the aerial tour, Tabitha wasn't sure which amenities to take advantage of, because immersing herself in local culture and learning about the island's history was her priority—aside from spending some time in a lounge chair on the beach while she attempted to relax, of course.

Elaine poked her shoulder. "You're holding up the line, my friend."

Shaking her head, Tabitha half-jogged down the gangway, weekender bag bouncing off her hip. "Sorry about that. Lost in my thoughts, I guess."

She stopped to receive her dual-cheek kiss from Quinton. He grinned, his hands grasping her upper arms. "Have a fabulous time. Remember, if you have questions or need any guidance with where to go or what to do, I'm staying right here on the island, so I'll be available at your disposal."

Tabitha smiled. "You're on speed dial." She paused, tilting her head. "Where is it you're staying? Just in case." "I'm at the Constance Ephelia. Semi-central Mahé, about eight miles from where you'll be. You folks are spread out all over the place, so I did my best to be in the middle." He let go of her arms. "Time to get moving. There's a van from Anantara Maia waiting to pick up guests. It's in the parking lot to your left. Just look for the logo."

"Thank you, Quinton," Tabitha nodded.

"You're welcome." He kissed Elaine's cheeks then waved her along. "Follow the leader, Elaine. She heard my spiel already. Enjoy yourself!"

Tabitha and Elaine spotted the van, not because of the logo, but because Doris was hopping up and down and waving at them from across the lot.

"Elaine! Tabitha! Over here!" She was clad in a wrap tank dress of khaki linen, a woven white sunhat, white wedge espadrilles, and white-framed round sunglasses that covered most of her face. "It's just us on this one, gals. The first van took the other ten residents who're staying at Anantara too. I'm so excited I can barely contain myself." Doris spun in a circle, her dress fanning out around her.

Elaine chuckled. "I'm not sure you're containing yourself, Doris. But I don't mind. Your enthusiasm is contagious." She spun around as well, stopped, then stared down at her white, knotted crop-top and Brunello Cucinelli capri jeans, shaking her head. "Not even half as much fun without a dress."

Tabitha glanced down at what she was wearing: purple polo shirt, khaki Banana Republic Explorer shorts, and black Alexander McQueen sporty triple-grip hiking sandals. She shook her head. "I'm not even going to bother to try. In part, because I'm also sans dress, but mainly because spinning tends to make me nauseated. Clapping is harmless, however."

She smiled and applauded as the van's driver opened the sliding side door and motioned them inside. They each sat in their own row to have a window all to themselves during the ten-mile ride from the Victoria port to Anantara Maia Seychelles Villas. Aside from an appreciative gasp or exclamation, the women remained quiet for the duration of the trip, focusing on the sights and scenery this slice of paradise had to offer.

⸱ℰ⸱ℯ⸱ℰ⸱ℯ⸱ℰ⸱ℯ⸱ℰ

The view from the bedroom of her beachside Villa left Tabitha speechless. She sat on the built-in, teak bench at the foot of the king-size bed, the upholstery, bedding, and canopy curtains bright white. Outside, a private deck and infinity pool gave way to an unobstructed view of the beach and the turquoise ocean beyond. On her right, beyond the bathroom, was an eight-by-eight outdoor soaking and hot tub next to the pool deck. Large teak columns supported a thatched roof, and on either side of the villa, wooden fences, brick walls, and a great deal of greenery provided maximum privacy.

The sound of the waves was the villa's most magical amenity, though. The ocean was less than fifty feet away, and Tabitha closed her eyes to listen to the waves crash on shore, an endless rhythm as old as time. It was a moment of immersive perfection, all sound and feeling.

The effect of the eighty-four percent humidity rate was best described as air you can wear, making the day's seventy-seven degree high seem much hotter than it was.

Cupertino, California's temperatures were similar, but the humidity topped out at sixty percent. Tabitha had little experience with tropical conditions, and she realized that all the clothes she'd brought with her might not be enough. Taking a deep breath, she stood up, then walked forward toward the pool. She shivered as a cool breeze hit her skin, then laughed.

"Ah, now I get it. The pool isn't just for swimming. It's nature's air conditioner," she said aloud. She studied the pocket doors designed to close off the bedroom from the deck. She decided to close them at night, at least until she got a handle on the flying insect situation.

After changing into her bathing suit, Tabitha exited the villa via the side door in the bathroom and walked barefoot across the grass toward the ocean. Doris and Elaine's villas were on either side of her, and both ladies were sitting in their lounge chairs on the beach, waiting for her. Their personal villa host, Adele, stood nearby behind a cart holding two bottles of champagne, three glasses, a charcuterie board, and a four-tiered arrangement of fruits and petit fours. Adele waved at Tabitha, and Doris and Elaine turned so they could see her.

Tabitha smiled and sighed happily as she nestled into the remaining lounger. Adele delivered their champagne, then returned to her post. The ladies held their glasses high in an unspoken toast, then immersed themselves in their surroundings. They remained on the beach until sunset, discussing their histories. Elaine had once been a model, and Doris was always involved in charity work. They also discussed their plans for the following days, and when darkness fell, they walked back to their villas together in the flickering torch light, bubbling with excitement about what lay ahead.

The ladies met at the reservation desk just after sunrise the next morning. Adele introduced them to Gabriel, their tour guide for the day. He escorted them to the guest van, then drove six miles down the road to the starting point of their journey. As he pulled into the parking lot, Tabitha pointed toward a row of vehicles located near the entrance of an oversize, bright-orange garage.

"Oh my gosh, look over there, ladies. Do my eyes deceive me or are those dune buggies?" Tabitha exclaimed.

Gabriel answered her question, glancing at the rearview mirror so he could make eye contact. "Yes, but we call them beach buggies here. That's our transportation for the day as we tour the island."

Doris clapped her hands. "Believe it or not, riding in a dune buggy is on my bucket list. I figured it would happen in a desert, but I like this option much better."

Elaine snorted. "Not on my bucket list, but I'm intrigued anyway. I've never seen a dune buggy in person, but I was rather fond of Schlepcar when I was young." The others looked confused. "You don't remember Schlepcar? It was on every Sunday morning, part of the . . . oh darn, that part's a bit fuzzy. Give me a minute." She paused, then held up her left index finger. "Got it! *The Krofft Supershow.* Schlepcar was like Herbie the Love Bug. A talking car, the sort of stuff that makes for both engaging children's television and frequent late-night visits to the parents' bedroom because of nightmares."

The group laughed as they exited the van and walked to the line of beach buggies. Gabriel pointed at a white four-seater with orange flames painted on its sides. "Hop in and buckle up, ladies. Our first stop is Port Glaud, where we'll park and take a short hike to Sauzier Waterfall."

Though bouncy, the beach buggy allowed the group to take the scenic route to Port Glaud, emerging from the jungle trail onto a long, narrow stretch of white sand beach. Tabitha pulled her iPhone from the pocket of her waterproof cargo shorts and captured a brief video of the small, wooden fishing boats swaying with the waves. The water was crystal clear, the sun reflecting off the scales of the school of blue tang swimming just off shore.

Gabriel drove up the beach, then turned onto Port Glaud's main road. Tabitha tried to take in every detail— the old stone churches, the island homes flanked by enormous palm trees, the way the sun warmed her skin, and the smell of salt air that awakened a hunger in her. But when Gabriel brought the buggy to a stop near the ticket booth for Sauzier Waterfall, it seemed that adventure was the answer, at least for now.

The hike to the falls took about five minutes, and the ladies had to navigate a stretch of rocky terrain before finding a spot across from the falls to sit. Gabriel took off his shirt and shoes and treated himself to a quick dip in the swimming hole at the foot of the falls. Tabitha, Doris, and Elaine took pictures and lost themselves in the sights, sounds, and smells of rushing water and the jungle's native fauna.

Once the sun dried Gabriel's skin, he donned his shirt again and led the group back to the beach buggy. They climbed aboard and headed for their next destination, the Mission Lodge Lookout in Morne Seychellois National Park, located five miles from the falls. The half-hour drive was uphill almost the entire way, and the ladies were glad for the opportunity to readjust to an upright position as they waited for Gabriel to return from the park office. He smiled as he handed them maps and informational brochures.

"Before we proceed, I'd like to share some local history with you." Making a sweeping gesture, he began. "The area surrounding the Lodge used to be known as Venn's Town. In the 1700s, children were brought here because their parents had been sold into slavery and taken to settlements. Missionaries built schools for them, provided them with an education, and prepared them for a life of freedom. They also advocated for the freedom of all those enslaved around the world. This spot, the highest point on the island, symbolizes that the ability to rise to great heights should be attainable by all. The work of the missionaries played such an important role in eradicating slavery that UNESCO declared the ruins of the village a World Heritage site, and it is an official Seychelles National Monument as well."

He began to walk, and the ladies followed, reaching the ruins in under ten minutes. The stone and brick remnants of each building were marked with informational plaques, and they stopped at each one, reading in silent reverence. At the far end of the trail stood a single marking stone, which their guidebooks described as the Liberated Slaves Cemetery Monument.

Gabriel allowed them time to process what they'd seen, then spoke. "Queen Elizabeth II visited this site in 1972." He pointed to his right. "She had her afternoon tea in that gazebo." He paused again, before continuing. "Now let's walk just a bit further so you can admire a view of Mahé unlike any other."

The Mission Lodge was located just below Sans Soucis summit, and as Tabitha stepped up to the viewing station, her mind went blank. All that existed was the beauty before her, the variegated greenery of the mountains, the cerulean ocean, the distant peaks of other islands visible through a curtain of haze. And the vibrant colors of the tropical birds as they flew above the lush canopy of flora that was their home. This place had been described as breathtaking, but she wasn't certain what that meant until this moment. Breathtaking and thought-taking as well. Doris's voice pulled her from her daze.

"My oh my, I may jest about my high hair bringing me closer to God, but this, ladies, is the real deal. I have never had the pleasure of seeing such majesty, aside from the faces of my little ones when I gazed upon them for the first time."

Elaine nodded. "I don't consider myself at all religious, but standing here is indeed a spiritual experience. I'm not sure I can put my feelings into words, honestly."

Tabitha turned to take in the view again. "I feel infinitesimally small and incalculably large all at once. What a privilege it is to experience this."

"You're right, Tabitha." Doris shook her head. "It's a shame that such things are unattainable for so many. Everyone should be able to stand here and feel what we're feeling right now."

"I agree, ladies," Elaine said. "The clarity this provides . . . we'll, it's humbling. No matter how much money we have, we're still just passing through. Short-term guests

on a rock that's been floating through space for four-and-a-half billion years." Elaine paused. "Do you ever think about it in those terms? How much money you have?"

Tabitha shook her head. "I hadn't until now. Between the three of us, we have a dollar for each year the earth has existed and then some. Wow. That's . . . wow."

Doris nodded. "That is a great big wow. I plan on leaving a large chunk to the children, and even with all my expenses factored in there's still lots left over. Hearing about the work that was done here by the missionaries made me think that it might be time to start giving back in some way."

"Same here, Doris." Elaine bit her lip. "I'm not sure where to start, though."

Tabitha smiled. "Ladies, break out your phones and start taking lots of pictures and videos up here and on the way back down. I have . . . an idea."

CHAPTER SIX

Seniors at Sea

Three hours later the ladies sat on Elaine's deck, sipping the mango, guava, and starfruit punch Adele had whipped up for them. She's added the KOHO rum they brought back from the Takamaka Distillery. It was the last stop on the beach buggy tour and served as another fascinating glimpse into not only the history of Mahé but the Seychelles themselves.

The family who owned the distillery began producing rum there in 2020, but their ancestors had settled on Mahé in 1772. One of the owners was kind enough to allow the group to record most of their tour on their phones. As they finished their first glass of what they dubbed Seychelles Shlosh, Tabitha decided it was time to reveal her plans to her friends.

She placed both hands on the round table Adele relocated from the lawn area so they could sit together. "Okay, gals. You were patient all day, for which I thank you, and I'm now tipsy enough to tell you my idea and survive possible embarrassment if you think it's ridiculous. So, ready?"

Elaine and Doris nodded. Tabitha cleared her throat. "I mentioned what a privilege it was to experience the view at the Mission Lodge, and Doris, you said everyone should be able to stand there and enjoy it. Both you and Elaine agreed that it might be time to give something back. What if giving back meant sharing our experiences with the world?" She paused to swallow. "I'm aware that travel blogs are a dime a dozen, and they're everywhere, but how many are curated by people who live on a cruise ship? And how many bloggers possess the financial resources we do? Resources that allow for the creation of quality content and extensive marketing and also provide access at no charge without an ulterior motive or agenda?"

Elaine and Doris didn't respond right away, and Tabitha mentally prepared herself to apologize. Just as she opened her mouth to begin, Doris pressed the palms of her hands together and grinned.

"Tabitha, I have no idea what this involves as far as the internet aspect, but I love it! Just tell me what I need to do and I'll do it."

Elaine bobbed her head in agreement. "I love it too, it's fantastic. I'll offer up funding and whatever skills I have. My blog design experience is minimal at best, but I know my way around social media and, if I do say so myself, I'm a darn good photographer. Those years as a model back in the late 80s and early 90s taught me more than how to strut down a catwalk with a smile on my face while wearing six-inch heels and pants that were creeping into places they had no business being."

The ladies all laughed, and Adele poured each of them another glass of Seychelles Slosh. Tabitha took two long sips, then spoke. "I have the structure of everything in my head, and I'm happy to do all the back-end work. If I'm honest, the one job-related thing I miss is having a project to work on, so this will be good for me from that angle. But there's one challenge I've yet to overcome. For the life of me, I can't come up with a name. Please help me out, won't you?"

Twenty minutes and forty-plus name options later, Doris jumped up from her chair, tipping it over behind her. "Oh, oh, I think I have it! How about—*Seniors at Sea*?"

Elaine's jaw dropped. "Doris, that's perfect." She turned to Tabitha. "Thoughts?"

Tabitha nodded. "I agree, it's perfect." She stood. "Ladies, I hate to be a party pooper, but my mind is buzzing with creativity, and I want to head back to my room and get the ball rolling." She grinned. "I might even pull an a haku lei all-nighter."

Doris wagged her index finger at Tabitha. "Don't you dare. We have big plans for tomorrow, Tabitha. There will be no falling asleep during the helicopter tour."

Tabitha shrugged as she walked into the villa, then paused to look back over her shoulder. "That's why God made coffee, ladies. So, we can do foolish things when the moon rises and still manage to enjoy ourselves after the sun comes up again."

C·c·C·c·C·c·C

It wasn't quite an all-nighter, but Tabitha decided three a.m. was close enough to brag about. She secured the domain name and created a WordPress blog, along with Twitter, Facebook, and Instagram accounts. Email invitations announcing the launch of *Seniors at Sea* were scheduled to go out to all Savannah Seas residents at eight a.m. local time, which she hoped would inspire everyone to share the information with their contact lists. Tabitha also made use of her own personal contacts, encouraging friends, family, and former colleagues to spread the word. She held off on reaching out to professional contacts for the time being, wanting to have more content available for visitors before calling in the big guns.

After sorting through all the footage from the day's travels, only three videos and fifty photos were usable, which wasn't bad, but she knew they could do better. This was new to them, but experience was the best teacher, and endless opportunities to hone their skills lay before them.

Yawning, Tabitha shut down her MacBook Air, intending to get up from the couch and shuffle off to the master bedroom. Instead, she fell asleep on the sofa and

remained there until her doorbell rang. Scared half to death, she jumped up, wincing at the crick in her neck. She walked to the door to see who was so deficient of manners that they'd wake someone up in the middle of the night. She checked the camera and was shocked to see Elaine and Doris standing in the hallway dressed in different clothes than earlier when she bid them goodnight. Rubbing her eyes, she realized it was far lighter than it should have been, which, combined with the neck pain, indicated that she might have been asleep much longer than she thought.

Tabitha unlocked and opened the door, squinting at her friends as they entered. "Please tell me it's not tomorrow already."

Doris made a tsk-tsk sound. "Looks like someone really did pull an all-nighter. For shame, young lady, for shame." She grinned. "Now show us what you've done, won't you? But make it snappy please. We only have forty-five minutes to get to the helicopter pad, and you need a shower and some coffee. From my vantage point, anyway." Elaine snorted.

"I agree. Your hair is doing some wild things, Tabitha. And not good wild. Though maybe a little punk rock is cool."

Tabitha interrupted her. "Yes, it does that. I tend to pull at it when I'm working. Give me a minute to boot up my laptop and put on some coffee. Then I'll show you everything."

Rolling her eyes, Doris walked past Tabitha and into the kitchen. "I'll make your coffee. You go have a shower, and then we'll take a gander, all right?"

Tabitha sniffed in the vicinity of her left armpit. "That's an excellent idea. Thank you."

She emerged fifteen minutes later wearing khaki cargo shorts and a light-gray polo shirt, her wet hair woven into a braid. Grabbing a banana from the kitchen island along with the coffee Doris poured into her silver to-go mug. Tabitha settled onto the couch in between her friends. The banana went down in four bites, and Tabitha set the peel on the coffee table, then picked up her MacBook Air. She took a long gulp of her coffee before speaking.

"Okay, ladies, here it is." Doris and Elaine scooted closer for a better view of the screen. "We have a blogging website where we can post detailed textual accounts of our adventures along with videos and photos, and I got us set up on Twitter, Facebook, and Instagram."

Tabitha gasped as she pulled up each social media service. "Oh my gosh, we've got 3,000 followers on Instagram and it's only . . ." She paused to glance at the MacBook's clock. "Nine o'clock. I set email invites to go out an hour ago, but only to 500 people."

The *Seniors at Sea* Facebook page had garnered just over 1,200 followers, with Twitter racking up 842. Doris used her phone to view the email Tabitha had sent and clicked on the Instagram link contained within it.

"Wow, the comments on the videos are lovely. Same thing on the photos. One person even said they'd always wanted to visit the Seychelles but hadn't managed to do so yet, but we made them feel like they were here with us. How wonderful!"

Elaine nodded. "Wow, that *is* wonderful." She reached into her backpack for her phone. "Facebook comments are similar. A few are asking if we plan to do a livestream at some point."

Tabitha tilted her head to the left. "Huh. That's an interesting idea. Hadn't thought about that until now. I think once we're in the swing of things, I'd like to give it a try."

"Speaking of getting in the swing of things, Tabitha, is what's posted the only usable footage from yesterday?" Elaine set her phone on the coffee table.

"You're correct, Elaine." When Doris and Elaine frowned, Tabitha shook her head. "Now, none of that. This is all new to us, and we'll get better at it as we go. Learning on the job, you know? That's the preferred way to do it. Experience is the best teacher."

Doris sighed, then smiled. "I can always ask my

grandkids to give us lessons. They're either watching TikTok videos or making them. One of them, Hunter, has 80,000 followers. He's fifteen. Most of what he posts are song parodies."

Elaine grinned. "Really? I'd love to take a look. I'm a huge Weird Al fan. Parodies are my jam."

Tabitha's stomach growled. "Oh, jam. I could go for some jam. On scones. Or toast. I'm not fussy. But I *am* hungry. Is food allowed on the helicopter, I wonder?"

Doris chuckled. "Tabitha, I'm relatively certain they'll let us bring whatever we want on the helicopter. We're the guests, remember?"

"The super-rich guests. They'd probably make a special stop for us to eat at a restaurant we saw from the air if we asked." Elaine stood. "Let's roll, ladies. It's time for our bird's eye view of Mahé."

Tabitha grinned. "And for our eyes to view the birds at the Aride Island Nature Reserve."

Doris was correct about food being allowed on the helicopter. Adele sent them off with a four-course picnic lunch, along with champagne to sip while they admired the sights. Elaine filmed takeoff, Tabitha filmed during the flight, and Doris shot footage the amphibious helicopter's touchdown off Aride Island. Despite being just over a mile long and a third of a mile wide, the island housed the largest number of seabird colonies in the Seychelles.

One passenger rowboat ferried the ladies to the beach, and a second brought the helicopter crew and their picnic lunch. A woman dressed in tan pants and a white V-neck T-shirt greeted them as they came ashore. Her close-cropped curly hair glistened in the sun.

"Greetings, ladies, and welcome to Aride Island Nature Reserve. My name is Coraline Tremblay, and I am the Sanctuary's resident veterinarian. Your hosts at Anantara have reserved the island exclusively for you for three hours today, and I will be your guide. Would you like to eat before or after the tour?"

All three answered "before" in unison, and Coraline chuckled. "Then eat you shall." She pointed at the young man who rowed their boat. "Thayer is my assistant. When you're finished, let him know and he'll escort you to my office."

Doris stepped forward. "Hello, Doctor Tremblay. I'm Doris, and this is Tabitha and Elaine" She pointed at each woman in turn. "If you aren't too busy, perhaps you, Thayer, and the rest of your staff would join us for lunch? Our host, Adele, packed enough food for a small army, and we'd love your company."

Coraline paused, the expression of surprise on her face shifting to joy in the blink of an eye. She laughed. "You know, it's ten years for me on this island, and I've never been asked that before. Thank you. It would be our pleasure to break bread with new friends."

Thayer led the group to three picnic tables situated to the left of the pathway into the jungle. Towering palm trees shaded the group from the hot sun as they dined on five-cheese, heirloom tomato, white truffle, and apple sandwiches; baby leaf salad with beluga caviar; Cornish crab and lobster with balsamic vinegar. For dessert, the Villa's chef prepared Ladob, a local dish containing plantains, cassava, and breadfruit soaked in coconut milk, sugar, nutmeg, and vanilla. Doris groaned when it was time to begin the tour. "How in the world am I supposed to walk around after all that food?"

Tabitha, already on her feet, extended her hand to help Doris up off the bench seat. "Come on, I know you can do it. Walking is the best thing for you after a large meal."

Elaine laughed. "She left out 'second only to a nap.' But she's right, you can do it. Today we're bird hunters and we need you, Doris Collins, to help flush 'em out and shoot 'em." She turned to Coraline. "Metaphorically speaking. After our excursion yesterday, we decided to start a travel blog. We're more like the bird paparazzi. Hunting with cameras only."

Tabitha grinned and held up her right index finger. "Posted for all the world to see on *Seniors at Sea*. Three thousand followers on Instagram and counting."

Coraline stroked her chin. "If you would like, I can tailor your tour to suit your purpose and serve as your narrator. As a non-profit, non-governmental organization, we rely on the generosity of the public to fund our facilities. Any opportunity to share our message and mission is deeply appreciated."

Doris, Elaine, and Tabitha glanced at each other, then gave enthusiastic nods. Tabitha spoke for all of them. "Coraline, we would be honored if you allowed us to film you narrating our tour. Thank you so much for suggesting it."

"I am so very pleased, Tabitha. It takes a great deal of money to maintain a nature reserve from a conservationist standpoint. Then there are the costs to ensure the animals remain in good health. Combined, they become an almost insurmountable challenge year after year. The more we are known, the better." Coraline gave a radiant smile. "Well, let us begin. I am ready for my closeup."

CHAPTER SEVEN

Next Port: Praslin

*U*pon returning to the Anantara Villa, Tabitha, Doris, and Elaine met for dinner in the Tec-Tec restaurant, phones at the ready. They chose a corner table that overlooked the beach, and sat admiring the sunset, sipping palm wine while reviewing the videos and photos they captured at the Aride Reserve. They paused for a dinner of local red snapper cooked in coconut milk with fresh chili, then resumed their efforts until Tabitha decided they had enough quality content for posting. Doris and Elaine sent her their files to upload on her own when she returned to her villa after dinner. Over cups of locally grown and produced Tropical Dream coffee, the three friends planned their final day on Mahé.

"What are your thoughts on visiting the Anantara Spa tomorrow?" Elaine sighed in delight as she took a sip of her Tropical Dream. "This right here is a darn fine cup of coffee."

Doris smiled. "It sure is, isn't it? And I'd love to make tomorrow a spa day. Have either of you looked to see what services they offer?"

Tabitha shook her head and Elaine nodded. "A Blue Diamond Facial, the Maia Signature Massage, and a Maia

Vichy Ritual. All for either sixty or ninety minutes, our choice."

Tabitha pulled up the Anantara Spa page on her phone and studied it for a moment. "Oh, that's what a Vichy Ritual is. It starts with a hydrotherapy treatment, followed by a full-body salt scrub, a massage with essential oils, a detoxifying body wrap, then a horizontal shower." She paused, tapping her lips with her right index finger. "Can we do all three, I wonder? Or is there such a thing as too many beautification treatments in a single day?"

Elaine shrugged. "I'm not sure about that, but I *am* sure that my preference is doing all three of them for the ninety-minute sessions." She waved Sophia, their server, over.

Sophia smiled. "How may I help you, ladies?"

"Sophia, we were wondering—can we do all three Anantara Spa offerings on the same day?" Elaine gazed up at Sophia, smiling in return.

"Yes, you can. Ideally, it's best do the Signature Massage and Blue Diamond Facial in the morning, then the Vichy Ritual in the late afternoon before dinner. Would you like me to book appointments for you?"

Tabitha nodded. "That would be wonderful, thank you. Please put us down for what you've suggested, reservations for four."

"I'll take care of that straight away. Is there anything

else I can get for you this evening?" Sophia held her hands out, palms up.

Tabitha shook her head. "We're all set. Thanks again. Dinner was delicious."

As Sophia walked away after bidding them good Mahé night, Elaine turned to Tabitha. "Reservations for four?"

"I thought we'd invite Captain Hopkins to join us, if she's able," Tabitha smiled.

Doris clapped her hands. "Tabitha, that's a lovely idea. I'm sure she could use a few hours away from the Savannah Seas. Hooray for a girls' spa day!"

Elaine glanced at the remainder of her palm wine. "I'd propose a toast, but I'm afraid if I have one more sip, you'll have to carry me back to my villa."

Tabitha laughed. "Same here. Verbal toast only, then. On my three. One, two—"

"To girls' spa day!"

Captain Hopkins joined them for the day, then returned to the Savannah Seas via the ship's tender after dinner on the beach. The ladies deemed the Vichy Ritual their favorite spa activity, and when Tabitha climbed into bed at nine, she felt more relaxed than she had in decades, if not ever.

The residents staying in hotels or villas on Mahé re-boarded the Savannah Seas at noon, and Captain

Hopkins began the two-hour voyage to Praslin at one-thirty. While enroute, Tabitha sat outside on her veranda, basking in the sunshine and breathing in the salt-laden ocean air. During stretches when no land was visible, she stared at the horizon, marveling that the view, while dynamic in actuality, appeared to remain static.

Tabitha stood so she could look overboard, but she was interrupted by her phone dinging to announce a new text message. Ding after ding followed as she pulled the device from the pocket of her gray hiking shorts. She pressed the wake button and was surprised to see the messages were all from Coraline Tremblay. Tabitha scanned them, creating a coherent paragraph in her mind from the short bursts on the screen.

'Hello Tabitha. Sorry to bother you. Big news from Aride to share. Since your posts we received many donations online. Almost half a million US dollars so far. Thank you from all of us.'

She read the texts five times over before the information jelled in her brain. Then realized she hadn't checked the *Seniors at Sea* follower counts since posting the Aride content. She pulled up Instagram and gasped.

"Fifty thousand followers? What the ever-loving heck is going on?" she said aloud. Facebook was next, and the findings were similar: 35,000. Twitter ran a close third with 28,000 following.

She called Elaine first to share the news, then Doris. Both were thrilled, but there wasn't time to get together to celebrate before they were due to dock at the Baie Sainte Anne port on Praslin. So, the ladies focused on repacking for their adventures over the next three days.

A guest car transported Doris, Elaine, and Tabitha to the check-in area of the Raffles Seychelles Hotel. They were accompanied to their individual Panoramic Pool Villas by a personal concierge who would provide them with round-the-clock service for the duration of their stay. Tabitha tipped Leo, her concierge, five $100 bills. As he thanked her, his expression remained pleasant but detached. But as he walked down the winding path back to the office, she heard him let out a whoop as he showed the tip to his co-workers.

Tabitha smiled and spoke aloud in the bright space of the combination living room-bedroom. "Glad I could make your day, Leo. And I can't wait to make you happy again tomorrow. And the next day."

The room's sliding doors were nestled in their pockets, providing Tabitha with an unobstructed view of the Indian Ocean beyond the private plunge pool and terrace sundeck. She walked outside, noting the covered pavilion to her left that contained a two-seat dining table and a daybed. The villa was located on a mountain, at the highest point on the hotel's property.

Tabitha was awestruck by the infinite shades of green and blue as far as the eye could see. She raised her arms and turned in a circle, taking in the panoramic view that earned the villas their name.

If I had realized such beauty existed, I would've walked away from Apple twenty years ago, Tabitha thought. *Samuel, I'm so sorry we never got to share this. I hope that somehow, wherever you are, you're aware of what I'm doing.*

She remained there, gazing at the ocean, along with her thoughts in the middle of paradise, until her phone alarm went off. She was meeting Doris and Elaine for dinner soon, and she needed to change into something more presentable than hiking shorts and an old T-shirt.

She opted for a white tank top and a black-and-white, paisley-pattern wrap skirt, slipped on her white Keds, then exited the villa and headed down the hill toward the Losean Restaurant. Much to her surprise, she was the first one to arrive, and the host led her to their reserved outdoor table. It was the farthest one from the building, set on the open seaside of a tropical garden. Three chairs were positioned on the garden-facing sides of the table, and an oversized patio umbrella shielded it from the late afternoon sun. Doris and Elaine arrived before Tabitha sat down, and Elaine whistled at the view as she approached.

"This must be a dream, right? We aren't really going

to spend the rest of our natural lives wandering around the world doing whatever we feel like, are we?"

Doris laughed. "Pinch yourself, darlin'. This is our reality now, and I love it. So much so that my kids have asked me to please stop thanking them via texts. I guess I'll just start sending pictures instead."

The ladies sat, and their server arrived within seconds. "Hello, ladies, and welcome to Losean. My name is Dahlia, and I'll be at your disposal this evening. Our specialty cocktail tonight is the Fun Fruity. It contains Coco d'Amour, which is a coconut liqueur made from coconut extract, bananas, papayas, mangoes, passion fruit, and oranges. Would you like to try one?"

The ladies nodded, and Dahlia distributed menus, then headed back inside to retrieve their drinks. Doris shook her head as she evaluated the available choices. "Someone else pick first, so I can copy your selection."

Elaine laughed. "Darn it, Doris. That was my plan too. But what the heck—I'll go for it. Tomato gazpacho soup and baby chicken salmi for me."

Doris wrinkled her nose in displeasure. "Well, now I know which two things I don't want."

Elaine shrugged, and Tabitha put her menu down. "Caprese salad and a ribeye steak for me."

Doris sighed. "That sounds delicious, but I promised myself I'd try to be more adventurous with my food choices.

I'm going to have the poached tiger shrimps in Takamaka dark rum and the pumpkin risotto."

Tabitha patted Doris's upper arm. "I'm very proud of you. I personally abhor everything pumpkin related."

Elaine affected an exaggerated West Coast millennial accent. "Oh my god, Tabitha, do you not like, like, pumpkin spice lattes? How is that even, like, possible? Next, you'll be saying you don't like Starbucks, either and then I'll have to unfriend you, like, everywhere. Even in, like, real life."

She stretched out the 'a' sound in "latte" and "Starbucks" for a solid two seconds, and the ladies were still doubled over laughing when Dahlia returned to take their order. They managed to compose themselves enough to speak for a few moments, then laughed all over again.

Dahlia delivered their meals twenty minutes later, and talk ceased as the ladies dug in. After dinner, they sipped coffee from clear-glass cups etched with palm leaves and outlined their plans for the next two days. Tomorrow, they'd visit Anse Lazio beach and do some snorkeling, and on the following day pay a visit to the Vallée de Mai Nature Reserve. Both locations were on all the Praslin "must see" lists, and would offer countless opportunities for filming. Tabitha texted Leo to ask if it was possible to acquire a GoPro Hero by morning, and he responded immediately with a thumb's up emoji. She held her phone in the air.

"We swim with the fishes tomorrow, my friends. Leo's

going to have a waterproof GoPro camera for us in the morning."

Doris sang the first verse of *Three Little Fishies*, and the other burst out laughing.

"Oh my gosh, my mother used to sing that to us kids whenever we drove down to the Jersey Shore," Elaine remembered. "My grandparents had a summer cottage on Long Beach Island, but the family sold it back in the 80s when my granddad moved into a care facility after my grandma died. They should've held onto it; the property sold for $2 million last spring." She shook her head. "It didn't occur to me to buy it then, but if it goes on the market again, I'm going to snap it up. It should remain in our family. We made so many memories there."

Tabitha reached out to pat Elaine's arm. "Nostalgia is a powerful thing. Don't wait until it's on the market. Contact the owner now, and make them an offer they can't refuse."

Elaine smiled. "Thank you, Tabitha. Sometimes, the concept that I'm a billionaire and can afford to purchase anything I desire eludes me. I'll have my attorney take care of it first thing tomorrow. The cottage means more to me than to the others. I think, because when we were there, my parents seemed happy. That wasn't often the case back in Pennsylvania." She frowned. "They divorced when I was sixteen. Dad didn't want me to become a model, but Mom thought it was the opportunity of a lifetime. I know there was much more to it than that, but it was the proverbial straw that broke the camel's back for their marriage."

Doris took a sip of her coffee, then raised her left index finger. "Elaine, none of that's on you. It's all on them. But yes, good god, get that cottage. You deserve it."

The sun set as the ladies finished their coffee. They exited Losean just as a three-seat rickshaw arrived to ferry them up the hill to their villas.

CHAPTER EIGHT

An Underwater Adventure

*A*nse Lazio beach was world renowned for its white sand and turquoise water, and the ladies hoped to use its reputation to their advantage. Doris stood ankle deep in the warm, wet sand as she captured a panoramic shot of the view capturing the expansive beach from the water.

"It's obvious why this is considered one of the most beautiful spots on the planet. It's like something out of a movie."

Elaine nodded in agreement. "And it might actually have been in a movie. I was doing some research last night for *Seniors at Sea* and learned that *For Your Eyes Only* was filmed in the Seychelles. Ian Fleming took a holiday here when he had writer's block and was fascinated by the pirate lore. Long story short, James Bond was probably right here at some point."

"You mean Roger Moore was probably right here," Tabitha grinned. "Not my favorite Bond, but he'll do."

Doris closed her eyes. "Now I'm picturing a shirtless Sean Connery running across the sand toward me, raring to save me from . . . from . . . uh, I don't think I care about that bit at all." She gasped. "Oh, he just picked me up and is running while carrying me . . ."

"Jeepers, Doris, you've got yourself the beginnings of a bodice-ripper romance right there." Tabitha chuckled; miming tearing open an invisible shirt. "My body is ready!"

Elaine laughed. "You two can share Sean, but I'm calling dibs on Pierce Brosnan."

Doris opened her eyes wide. "Number one, there will be no Sean sharing in my fantasy, young lady. Number two, we've gotten ourselves way off track. I've always wanted to go snorkeling, and for my first time, to be in a place like this with friends like you . . . what a precious gift."

Elaine and Tabitha linked arms with Doris, then walked back to the spot on the beach where they'd left their equipment.

They chose to explore the South Zone first, and Tabitha's first underwater video was of a series of granite blocks that looked like someone had dropped them in the sand just offshore. The water remained clear as they swam out further, surrounded by groups of steel pompanos and white sergeant major fish with black and yellow stripes.

Angelfish, bluefin trevallies, and hawksbill sea turtles also made appearances, the turtles starring in a five-minute video so moving Tabitha's goggles fogged over with tears. When the group reached the shark protection netting area, they returned to the beach and walked down to the North Zone.

The water in the North Zone wasn't as deep as the South, which allowed the rocks to be more abundantly colonized by coral. Tabitha marveled at the electric-blue damselfish as they swam in small groups among individual reef needlefish, weaving in and out between them. A bit further out, a large school of lined surgeonfish moved as one between her and Elaine, shifting and flitting in a wave-like motion, their iridescent bellies flashing in the midday sunshine. It was hypnotic, and Tabitha let the water take her where it pleased.

Out of the corner of her eye, she saw Elaine wave, then point down. Tabitha glanced toward the spot and saw nothing unusual—then the sand shifted and a stingray emerged, its yellowish skin covered in blue polka dots. Had the online, marine-life identification guide mentioned stingrays? She couldn't remember. She resisted the urge to touch it, remembering that The Crocodile Hunter, Steve Irwin, was killed by a stingray barb.

Elaine waved and pointed again, and Tabitha saw at least seven rays to their immediate left. The ladies swam to the right, moving slowly to avoid alarming the rays. Once they got about fifteen feet away, Tabitha and Elaine nodded to each other and pointed toward the shore. At that moment, Tabitha realized Doris wasn't with them, and her heart lurched. But when they finally reached the shore, they found Doris standing in the sand, just out of reach of the tide, her right hand over her heart.

"Thank God you're both okay!" she cried out. "I got way ahead of you somehow, and while I was looking for you, I saw a man pet one of the rays. It tried to swim away, but the man grabbed one of its fins, so it stung him. I yelled for help and the lifeguard dove in, swam to the fellow, then dragged him back the beach. I'm surprised you didn't hear him howling even though you were under water."

Doris shook her head. "Some people just don't understand that you look with your eyes, not with your hands. When you're in the water, you're a guest in their home and need to be respectful."

Elaine grimaced. "So, is he, you know . . . okay? Or is he . . ."

Doris rolled her eyes. "He'll be fine. The lifeguard said that blue-spotted, ribbon-tail rays do have venom, but it isn't powerful enough to kill a human. It hurts like the dickens, however, which I hope teaches him a lesson." She frowned. "I was worried about you two, though. Not that you'd try touching a ray, but that they'd be riled up and attack you. I'm very glad you're both safe and sound."

Tabitha blew out a breath. "Thank you, Doris. Tell you the truth, I was tempted to touch one of those creatures

myself. Glad I was able to control my impulse, that's for sure."

Elaine chimed in. "Me, too. There must be a place somewhere in the Seychelles where we can do so safely. Like an aquatic petting zoo, maybe?" She reached for her phone, laughing when she connected with a wet bathing suit instead. "Why yes, I was indeed going to search for an aquatic petting zoo while standing on one of the most pristine beaches in the world with an ocean teeming with marine life right in front of me." She shook her head. "There's one close to where I lived in Pennsylvania. The Aquarium in Scranton if I recall correctly. I used to walk the mall it's in. There are stingrays on the mural painted near the entrance."

"Wait, did you say Scranton? As in home to the Dunder Mifflin Paper Company Scranton? *The Office* Scranton?" Tabitha's eyes widened with excitement.

Elaine nodded. "Well, sort of. They did film a few things there to get the setting correct for the show's intro, but everything else was shot on the West Coast, from what I understand. After the divorce, I always mentioned Scranton when someone from back home in New York wanted to know what the closest city to me was. Most of them asked if I visited Dunder Mifflin. Occasionally I said yes, just for funsies."

Tabitha grinned. "I love that show so much. It's spot on regarding what it's like to work in an office. Granted,

Apple was a high-pressure environment, but we had our share of Dwights, let me tell you. The only difference is that we were focused on code instead of beets."

Doris glanced Tabitha to Elaine and back again. "I'm afraid I have no frame of reference. I've never seen the show. Perhaps you'll watch it with me when we're back on the Savannah Seas?"

Tabitha and Elaine nodded, and they walked with Doris back toward the South Zone to have lunch at Le Chevalier Bay. After they finished, Tabitha called the hotel to request a pickup, and the car arrived ten minutes later. The ladies parted ways when they returned to the hotel, Doris and Elaine tasked with sending their videos and photos to Tabitha so she could post same-day content.

Watching the footage of the hawksbill sea turtles made Tabitha weep with joy, and she decided it should be the Anse Lazio collection's showpiece. She searched a few royalty-free music websites, but nothing seemed to fit. After an hour, she took a break, hoping that walking away would give her a fresh perspective.

The sun rested low on the horizon, and Tabitha sat on the edge of the private plunge pool and dangled her feet in the water. The temperature was perfect, not too hot, not too cool. She contemplated taking a swim but was too lazy to get up and put on a bathing suit. She glanced around, evaluating just how "private" her private quarters were.

"Hmmm, private enough," she thought. "I can't see anyone else, so I guess they can't see me. I'm sure people have swum here in the buff before. Why not me too?"

She stripped off her clothes and threw them on the deck, sighing as she sank into the water. "Guess I can check skinny dipping off the bucket list," she thought. She remained in the plunge pool as the sun set, enjoying the view and the joyous peace it brought her.

And then, inspiration struck. Tabitha hopped out of the pool, swept up her clothes, and ran to the bathroom to dry off and change into a plush, Turkish cotton robe. Then she said on the couch, MacBook Air balanced on her knees. After a few clicks, Beethoven's *Ode to Joy* was playing in perfect sync with the movements of the turtles. She uploaded the file and posted it on all the *Seniors at Sea* accounts, smiling as tears ran down her cheeks.

She spoke aloud, "This one's going to be a big hit. I can feel it."

Doris wished she'd worn something other than flip-flops as she half-jogged down the hill to Elaine's villa, hoping she'd arrive before Tabitha. They'd decided last night to meet there for breakfast. But Doris had overslept, because, as her grandkids liked to say, her phone had been "blowing up" with notifications into the wee hours. She turned them off just after three-thirty a.m. but neglected to set her wake-up alarm. By a stroke of luck, she woke on her own at eight-thirty, only fifteen minutes later than usual. She rushed through her morning routine, attempting to brush her teeth while checking the *Seniors at Sea* Instagram account and almost dropping her phone into the sink.

She could see Elaine's porch now, and as she got closer, both Elaine and Tabitha came outside to greet her, grinning from ear to ear. They'd obviously seen the good news, too.

Tabitha cupped her mouth and shouted, "Half a million and counting on Instagram! Facebook, too!" She shrugged as Doris joined her and Elaine on the porch. "Twitter's only at 83,000. Not our target market, it appears."

Doris crossed her arms and pouted. "Darn it, I wanted to turn up early and surprise you with the news." She smiled. "But that doesn't matter, because this is amazing and I'm tickled all shades, not just pink."

Elaine nodded with enthusiasm. "Me too. The turtle video really struck a chord with people. It's even being reposted on other platforms like Tumblr and TikTok. With proper credit given to us, in most cases."

"It was a surreal experience, swimming with them," Tabitha said, sinking into one of the bamboo porch chairs. "They're living fossils, still the same after millions of years from an evolutionary perspective, residing in the same

physical space. They were here before humans, and they'll be here after we're gone. It's like reaching through time and touching the past, in a way."

"Yes, you've hit the nail on the head there, Tabitha. It's akin to staring into infinity." Elaine shuddered. "Gosh, that gave me chills."

"Prepare yourself for additional chills, because from what I've read, Vallée de Mai may have the same effect on you. The palm forest there hasn't changed at all since dinosaurs were cruising around the Seychelles." Tabitha chuckled. "There's a joke in there somewhere about our ages, but if I make one, I'm afraid a velociraptor will leap out from behind a tree and . . . well, you know what happens next."

Doris smirked. "A major motion picture studio offers you a six-movie deal?"

"The velociraptor is offered a job as a mascot for an international insurance provider?" Elaine snorted at her own humor.

Tabitha rolled her eyes, then laughed. "Wow, we're all in excellent spirits today ladies, and who could blame us? Let's have some breakfast and get moving."

The trip to Vallée de Mai took fifteen minutes, and the guest van driver provided the ladies with his cell phone number so they could reach him whenever they were ready to return to their villas. Before driving off, he retrieved their backpacks from the rear cargo area, then pointed in the direction of the visitors center. It was a short walk up a well-traveled trail, and after purchasing tickets, the ladies stopped in the locker area to change into hiking-appropriate footwear. They also secured credit cards, cards, jewelry, medications, spare eyeglasses, and other items in a shared locker they didn't want to risk losing in the palm forest. Elaine helped Doris adjust her backpack's straps, and then they were off to meet their guide.

Up ahead, a tall man with a long black braid and wearing a bright-green shirt with a white, Vallée de Mai logo waved, then walked to meet them.

"Greetings, friends! My name is Antonio, and I'll be your guide as we walk the palm forest trails today. Would you prefer the one-mile or the two-mile journey?"

Tabitha, Doris, and Elaine opted for the two-mile tour, and Antonio proved to be a font of both historical and scientific information. He offered facts about the featured trail stops and more details upon request, including the fact that most of the forest consisted of coco de mer palms. Halfway through their expedition, Antonio paused at a way station. The three-sided structure contained long tables upon which several large, wooden, sculpture-like items rested.

Elaine pointed at them. "Antonio, what the heck are those things?"

Doris tilted her head to one side. "Is it me, or do they look like carvings of someone's rear-end?"

Antonio's laughter rang out. "I get that question a lot, Doris. Yes, they do. Others see them as hearts."

Tabitha raised her hand. "That's exactly what I thought! I most certainly did not sing the chorus of *Baby's Got Back* in my head as soon as I saw them. Not at all."

"Now that's a new one, Tabitha. I will add it to my repertoire." Antonio smirked, then gestured toward the tables. "Those are, believe it or not, seeds from the coco de mer palm trees."

Elaine gasped. "No way, seriously? They're enormous."

Antonio nodded. "Yes, they are. Some have weighed more than ninety pounds, which, when we consider that the trees themselves are a hundred feet tall with leaves that average between twenty and thirty feet long, seems appropriate. They are unique to the Seychelles, and when Praslin was discovered, this forest was thought to be the Garden of Eden.

"The truth is that when the continents split, the Seychelles were isolated and remained undisturbed until modern times. Much like on Madagascar, evolution here took a different path, one without human interference. There are several unique species of animals on Praslin, including the black parrot. When coco de mer palms die, the black parrots nest in their remains. We'll probably see a few as we head back to the visitors center, and if we're lucky perhaps we'll also come across some bronze geckos, blue pigeons, or Seychelles chameleons. I'll let you know when I spot any native fauna."

True to his word, Antonio located all the animals he'd mentioned and more, and the ladies took so many photos and videos that they almost maxed out the storage on their phones. Tabitha used the GoPro for the final leg of the walk, focusing on the coco de mer palms and their double-nut seeds.

On the ride back to the Raffles Hotel, the women sat in silence scrolling through the photos they captured that day. Once again, Tabitha felt a powerful connection to the past, to something both ancient and timeless. It freed her spirit.

When she dozed off in bed later that night, her MacBook Air still open and connected to the internet resting next to her on the bed, she dreamed of walking through a prehistoric forest with Samuel by her side, the sun's rays penetrating the palm leaves and shining on their upturned faces.

CHAPTER NINE

Final Port: La Digue

abitha, Elaine, and Doris returned to the Savannah Seas the following morning and reconnected with the other residents over brunch. Lorenzo expressed his delight with the *Seniors at Sea* endeavor, as did most in attendance. Several people were interested in participating, and the trio agreed to discuss the matter after the Seychelles adventure was completed.

Their final stop was the island of La Digue, and the Savannah Seas docked at the port of La Passe at six p.m. Housing on the island was limited, and motorized vehicles were not permitted, so most residents opted to remain on the ship and use the ship's tender or the island's ferry service.

The ladies, however, decided to book three, sea-front deluxe rooms at the Le Nautique Luxury Waterfront Hotel. It was centrally located and offered unparalleled views. Mountain bikes were available to all Le Nautique guests for a nominal fee, and the ladies reserved theirs when they checked in.

After unpacking, the three friends dined at the hotel's waterfront restaurant. Tabitha and Doris ordered the evening's special, madras chicken and garlic naan, while

Elaine chose rogan josh, a similar dish made of lamb instead of chicken.

Doris never tasted curry before, and when the heat flared after the first bite of chicken, her eyes watered and she fanned her face with her hands. "Good lord, when they say curry is spicy, they mean it. This is like the hot flashes I had when I was going through menopause. Hoo boy!"

Tabitha pointed to a bowl filled with a white, creamy substance in the center of the table, next to a platter of plain naan. "That's cucumber raita, I think. Dip some of the naan into it and take a bite. It will help, trust me." She smiled. "The regular naan, not the garlic naan. That would be like pouring gasoline on a fire." Doris dipped the bread and took a bite, sighing with relief within seconds. "Oh, that's better. And wow, it's delicious. Thank you, Tabitha."

Tabitha nodded. "You're welcome. Samuel loved Indian cuisine. We ordered takeout from his favorite place at least twice a week. They were open until midnight, which worked well with our schedules." She frowned. "All that time I spent as someone's employee seems . . . well, wasted, I guess. Especially considering what we've experienced here in the Seychelles. This planet holds so many treasures for us to discover, yet we shoehorn ourselves in tiny pockets of it instead of exploring."

Elaine patted Tabitha's hand. "What you're leaving out is that exploring costs money. Which, unless you're very

fortunate, requires work to obtain. Or a well-constructed divorce settlement." She grinned, then sobered. "Listen, all that matters is that you're exploring now. You're doing it! And you're sharing your experiences with others. How wonderful is that?"

Tabitha nodded, the corners of her mouth turning up in a slight smile. "It's off-the-charts wonderful. Thank you, Elaine. It's just, sometimes I—"

"Sometimes you second guess the choices you made and lose yourself in a 'what if' scenario," Doris said. "It happens to all of us. Some days, I miss Buck so much, part of me wishes we'd opted for a middle-class lifestyle where he could've spent more time with our family instead of focusing on growing our net worth. But then I remind myself all I have the power to change is my future, not my past." She snorted. "And one change I'm making right now is adding some of that cucumber raita to every bite of my madras chicken, so I don't spontaneously combust."

The ladies laughed their way through the rest of dinner. Afterward, they decided to discuss their plans for tomorrow while walking on the beach. The moon was almost full, and the white sand sparkled like diamonds under their feet. When talk of activities waned, they sat down, sifting handfuls of sand through their fingers, enjoying each other's company and the rhythmic sounds of the waves. New friends who hoped to be friends for life.

~·~·~·~·~·~·~

L'Union Estate, a vanilla and coconut plantation, was just over a mile from Le Nautique, so the ladies decided to utilize the mountain bikes instead of walking. They spent fifteen minutes in the hotel parking lot reacquainting themselves to the bike-riding process. Elaine was the only one who'd ridden a mountain bike, so she served as their instructor. Tabitha and Doris adapted quickly, both commenting that the bikes were much easier to shift than old-school, ten-speeds.

The bike trails were impressive, a slice of urban modernity amid an otherwise untouched landscape. Made from concrete and wide enough for four bikes to fit next to each other, they allowed cyclists to travel at their own pace with minimal risk of encroaching on other riders' personal space and causing an accident. It took only seven minutes to bike to L'Union, and after dismounting, they locked their bikes on the rack near the ticket center. No personal guides were available. But the counter clerk assured them that the Estate's signage was designed for self-guided touring, although staff members were posted along the way to answer questions or address concerns.

A short distance from the ticket center they encountered a cluster of small homes to the right side of a cemetery. Tabitha waited until Elaine was ready to

shoot a video, then read the text of the sign out loud to her companions.

"The first settlers of La Digue came from Reunion and Mauritius in the late eighteenth century. They made their homes here, which have been carefully restored and maintained. The graves of the founders can be found in the cemetery to your left." She glanced toward the cemetery, noting the stark whiteness of the headstones and monuments against the greenery of the surrounding flora and the striking blue of the cloudless sky. The ocean was visible in the near distance. "Well, I've got to say, as far as a final resting place goes, this one is at the top of the list."

Doris nodded. "I agree. It's so beautiful and peaceful. Are we allowed to go inside the houses, do you think?"

Tabitha shrugged. "The sign doesn't say we can't, so let's go for it."

It was humbling for the women to imagine the trials and tribulations the original settlers endured as they made La Digue their home, but it was understandable why they'd come here, worked so hard, and persevered. It a very literal sense, this was paradise on earth.

The next stop was a traditional copra factory, according to the sign. A smiling staff member greeted them, her dark, curly hair pulled back in a ponytail.

"Hello, there! My name is Adrienne. Would you

like me to show you how coconuts were processed to create coconut oil before the industrial revolution?"

Elaine nodded. "I was just about to Google 'copra factory' so yes, please. Right, ladies?" Doris and Tabitha nodded as well. "Would you mind if we take videos while you give us the tour?"

Adrienne grinned. "Not at all. Follow me, please." She led them to a hut containing a long table and a huge pile of coconuts. "The coconuts were husked here, then the husks gathered and put to the side. The next step was breaking open the coconuts and removing the white part, which is called the flesh. As you can imagine, that was quite a dangerous process when performed with rudimentary tools."

Next, she led them to what looked like a large oven. "They placed the harvested flesh in this kiln, and used the coconut husks along with wood as a fire source. Then they brought the dried flesh, called copra, to the mill over there." She pointed to a large, well-worn cylindrical stone set in the ground under an open-air structure with a thatched roof. "An ox or bull served as the energy source for milling. Around eighty pounds of copra was needed to fill a one-gallon pail with coconut oil."

Elaine stopped recording, and Tabitha emitted a low whistle. "Wow, that's a lot of coconuts. How long did it take to mill that much copra?"

"Several hours, depending on the speed of the animal."

Adrienne extended her arms from her sides, palms facing upward. "Any other questions you'd like me to answer?"

Doris, Elaine, and Tabitha shook their heads, then thanked Adrienne for her time. They walked for several minutes before coming across a large, wooden house with a thatched roof. Doris reached the sign first and read the text aloud as Elaine recorded her.

"This plantation house was erected by the Hossen family in the early nineteenth century. It is one of the oldest structures featuring French colonial design in the Seychelles. Coconut farming was the main export crop of La Digue, and the plantation still serves as a source for both coconuts and vanilla."

Tabitha photographed the home from all angles, and the ladies walked through both the coconut and vanilla plantation areas. There were several picnic tables near a gift shop just outside the vanilla plantation, and the ladies decided this was the perfect spot to break for lunch. Le Nautique offered to-go meals on request, and the chef prepared jambon-beurre for them and packed it in a small, portable cooler. Comprised of half a baguette loaded with salted French butter, sliced Jambon de Paris ham, Gruyère cheese, and Dijon mustard, the ladies expected it to be rather ordinary, but one bite revealed it to be an exceptional sandwich, the perfect blend of flavors.

After cleaning up and using the restroom, they

continued walking the trail. They knew the Anse Source d'Argent Beach was located on the far side of the plantation but were surprised to hear the sound of waves crashing less than a hundred feet from where they'd just eaten.

Tabitha tilted her head. "I can't believe we're almost at the beach. My brain is having a difficult time processing the fact that islands are, well, islands. I mean, I'm used to being close to the water but more so in a 'get in the car and drive there' way. The water here is . . . everywhere, which I'm enjoying. But—oh my God, is that what I think it is?" She pointed up ahead and to the right.

Doris squinted. "If what you think you're seeing is an enormous tortoise, then yes, it is."

Elaine used her phone to zoom in. "Enormous doesn't quite cover it, but yeah. Tortoise."

Tabitha started jogging toward it, with Elaine and Doris following behind. As they got closer, they saw a young woman guide on duty. She waved them over. "My name is Mikos, and this is a tortoise enclosure. These are Aldabra giant tortoises, native to this area of the Seychelles and one of the largest species of turtles in the world. Adults can grow as large as five feet tall, four feet long, and weigh more than 500 pounds. Their lifespan is estimated at around 200 years." Mikos explained that lifespan was difficult to authenticate, because the tortoises lived almost twice as long as the humans tasked with tracking them.

"You're lucky. You showed up at snack time. Do you want to feed the tortoises bananas?" Mikos asked.

They nodded in unison. Doris sat on a large rock next to a giant fellow named Francois and watched as he took a bite, masticated in a thoughtful way for a minute, then took another bite. It looked up at Tabitha, who'd already exhausted her supply of bananas. "It's like watching a stop-motion, prehistoric creature feature from back in the day. He's so slow, but then when it's time for the next bite, he moves like lightning. Well, tortoise-speed lightning. It's jarring when you're staring at him the whole time, though."

"I never knew I held such a fondness for Testudines," Doris smirked. "I've been researching. Thank you, Google. Turtles are an aquatic species, and tortoises are a terrestrial species." The smirk became a grin. "And now I feel like the dad from *My Big Fat Greek Wedding,* with his word origin lectures."

"Turtle, tortoise, there you go." Elaine chuckled. "Not quite etymology, but close enough to be hilarious."

They waved at Mikos and the tortoises as they walked away toward Anse Source d'Argent. As they reached the end of a short dirt trail and entered a dense palm forest, the trio gasped in unison.

Elaine spoke first. "I feel like I'm either on another planet or I've travelled back in time. Look at those granite boulders, good god. I read that they were amazing, and I saw pictures but . . . wow. I was not at all prepared, my friends."

The Anse Source d'Argent Beach, though small, was at the top of the "world's most beautiful beaches" list. White sand and turquoise water were ordinary beach features in the Seychelles, but the rock shoreline was unlike anything on earth. Exposure to the elements had sculpted the striated, black-granite boulders into smooth works of art over millions of years. It was breathtaking.

The ladies spent the better part of an hour filming and taking photographs. Afterward, they walked arm in arm back to the ticket center to retrieve their bikes. Tomorrow, they decided they'd spend the day riding their bikes around La Digue. No plans, no agenda, no structure. A day to immerse themselves in their surroundings and local culture; a boots-on-the-ground glimpse of life in paradise for the three of them and their *Seniors at Sea* followers.

CHAPTER TEN

Turning Tides

The first night back on the Savannah Seas felt odd to Tabitha, and she was unsure of where she was when her eyes opened the following morning. They were still moored off the Seychelles and planned to dock on Mahé to pick up some supplies before setting sail again.

By the time she finished showering, she was back in the swing of things and ready to meet her friends at Day n Night, the ship's restaurant that served nothing but breakfast food twenty-four hours a day, seven days a week. She turned off her phone the night before so she wouldn't be tempted to compulsively check in with her friends, but she decided to turn it back on in case their plans had changed. The device emitted non-stop notifications for almost a minute once it connected to the ship's wi-fi, and Tabitha checked texts from Elaine and Doris before looking at anything else. She read their messages four times, set the phone on the counter, and then sank onto the couch, feeling like she might pass out.

After a brief session of meditative breathing, Tabitha stood, raised her hands in the air and screamed, "A million followers! *Seniors at Sea* hit a million followers!"

The elevator ride down to deck seven seemed to take a year, and when the doors opened, Elaine and Doris were waiting for her. They screamed, threw their arms around each other, and jumped up and down chanting "million follower group hug", until they heard another elevator ding, announcing the arrival of other residents.

They took off for Day n Night so they wouldn't have to greet whomever it was, asked the hostess for a booth in the back, then sat and tried to maintain some semblance of decorum. Success had given them healthy appetites, and Tabitha ordered a bacon, egg and cheese wrap; Doris, a stack of buttermilk pancakes; and Elaine, eggs sunny-side-up with sausage and rye toast. By the time coffee arrived, the women felt calm enough to discuss the exiting new development without making a scene.

Tabitha leaned forward, whispering, *"Seniors at Sea* has a million followers."

Elaine nodded, also whispering. "On Instagram and Facebook. I didn't check Twitter. I don't care about Twitter."

Tabitha gave her a thumbs up. "Me neither. It's not a good platform for what we're doing. It's impossible to convey what we see in so few characters."

Doris put her palm to her forehead. "Ladies, I just remembered—I came across something that I thought was very interesting last night, and I fell down a rabbit hole

reading everything there. Which is probably why I almost forgot to mention it." Their food arrived, and Doris held up her right index finger. "It can wait until after we eat, but please, please remind me."

"I don't want to wait, but my stomach says I should, so yes. I'll remind you," Elaine said. She salted her eggs and dipped her toast into the yolks.

The wait wasn't a long one, and as soon as their server cleared the dishes and replenished their coffee, Elaine patted Doris on the hand and stared into her eyes. "Okay, Doris. I'm reminding you. Let's hear it."

Doris took a deep breath and blew it out. "Well. I hope this doesn't sound strange, but when Buck was sick, I joined some online groups. Retired people with a spouse living with cancer or dementia or having mobility issues, things like that. It was nice to talk to other folks in a similar situation, and it helped me cope and to be a better caregiver for Buck. Anyway, when he passed, I stopped interacting, but last night one of the gals from the group sent me an email invite to a different group. She said she thought I should check it out because she saw some photos and videos of me there. I was confused because I don't usually post such things online, and then it dawned on me that it might be about *Seniors at Sea*. And sure enough, when I clicked the link and joined, there it was—the *Seniors at Sea* Discussion Group."

Tabitha's eyes went wide. "No way."

Doris nodded. "*Yes* way. And I have to tell you, what I read . . ." She placed her right hand over her heart. "It was indescribably moving. It's a group of retirees from around the globe who aren't able to travel due to health issues or other circumstances, but they're able to live vicariously through our experiences, and it means so, so much to them. Every post made me cry. They're so full of joy and so grateful and . . ." Tears rolled down Doris's cheeks, and Tabitha slid closer and put an arm around her friend's shoulder.

Elaine reached across the table to take Doris's hand. "How about we go up to Tabitha's place, and you can show it to us on her laptop?"

Tabitha nodded. "I can cast the screen to the television, so we don't huddle over and end up in the ship's ER with our backs out."

Doris wiped her eyes, then laughed, and the others joined in. They left a $300 tip for their server, then headed to the elevators.

Four hours flew by as they went through the discussion group's posts, taking frequent breaks to compose themselves after reading one that tugged at their heartstrings. A member named Eleanor was ninety-five, and while still mobile, she was no longer allowed to drive

and resided in a senior living community in Vermont. She'd travelled frequently in her younger days, and out of all the changes in her life, not being able to do so any longer hit her the hardest. Her all-caps comment, I CAN FEEL THE WATER ON MY SKIN on the swimming turtle post. It stood out above all others!

Ricardo was sixty-eight and had just lost his wife after a ten-year battle with breast cancer that left him bankrupt and living with his eighty-nine-year-old mother. He said the images of the Liberated Slaves Monument and the view from the Mission Lodge Lookout on Mahé gave him hope and inspired him to keep moving forward. He now had a goal: to see these sites in person before he died.

Stephanie suffered a stroke three years before and was confined to a wheelchair. She required multiple accommodations to browse the internet, and typing was impossible. Her aide was so impressed by the positive change in her attitude in Stephanie's attitude after reading the group's posts, that she volunteered to do the typing on Stephanie's behalf so she could interact with the other members.

There were many more posts, but what impacted the ladies most of all were the friendships that had formed within the group. Tabitha glanced up at the ceiling, then at Doris and Elaine in turn before speaking.

"Ladies, how do you think the *Seniors at Sea* Discussion Group would feel about one of us joining?"

Doris's mouth opened, then closed. "Oh, Tabitha, that's brilliant. I'd like to volunteer to take that on if it's okay with both of you."

Tabitha laughed. "I was hoping you'd say that. If you join, you can post all our content right there, so the members don't have to go looking for it to repost or link to."

Elaine shook her head. "I honestly cannot believe this is happening. I thought it would be fun, you know, to post stuff and have followers. But this, I can't quite articulate how it's making me feel other than . . . more. Does that make sense? Nah, it doesn't make sense. I should just—"

"Sure, it makes sense," Tabitha said, standing up and pacing. "We started on this journey intending to spend our retirement cruising around the world, constantly on the move, calling this floating palace our home. Luxury and relaxation with a bit of exploration mixed in. And then, for a short time, we thought we'd lost it all. But we didn't, instead, we wound up owning it all. That sort of thing changes your perspective, or at least it did for me."

Doris and Elaine nodded in agreement, and Tabitha continued. "Then we arrived on Mahé, and like Ricardo, we saw the monument and the view from the lookout, and in

that moment we all realized that there was—like you said, Elaine—more. More than cruising. More than luxury. More than relaxing. Our desire to share our adventures with the world meant that we were searching for something, even though we didn't consciously realize it at the time. We were searching for meaning, for purpose, to form a connection outside ourselves with the world at large. A joyful way to celebrate not just our own lives, but the lives of everyone we encounter on our journeys, as well as those who share in our journeys vicariously. And ladies, guess what? We've done it all. And I'd like to keep doing it. How about you?"

Doris and Elaine leapt to their feet as they shouted "yes," then pulled Tabitha into an embrace.

Later that evening, Tabitha stood alone on her veranda, gazing out over the ocean. The sky was clear, the moon was full, and the ocean sparkled like a sapphire. She understood Samuel now more than she ever had when he was alive, why he chose to travel and capture images, no matter the place or the circumstances. His work documented history, but it also documented emotions—joy, sorrow, terror, exultation, love, and hate. Also, life and death. The delicate balance of humanity on an ever-shifting tightrope. Images frozen in time, allowing future generations to discover the world around them and something about themselves, as well.

Tomorrow, the residents of Savannah Seas would learn about their next destination. Tabitha smiled, caring not a whit about where they ended up, only that they'd be going.

EPILOGUE

aptain Charlotte Hopkins stood on deck four of Savannah Seas, watching the brightly clad residents parade down the gangplank at Port Miami. The ship had docked the night before, and today, most of the 250 cruisers had disembarked to spend the day touring Miami. They had a one-week layover before their next launch, and luckily, there was a lot to see in the vibrant city.

Charlotte smiled to herself as she observed most of the residents climbing into the limos idling at the curb. Chauffeur service was just one of the many amenities provided by Savannah Seas. Every day, residents would shuttle from South Beach to Little Havana, to Zoo Miami, to the Bayside Marketplace, and to other attractions, then be transported back to the ship in time to rest up and change for a five-course dinner. While the crew had some much-needed time off, the meals on board were catered by the finest restaurants in the area and special services were hired for a top-to-bottom cleaning of the magnificent ship. What a life.

Charlotte chose the Azores, nine mid-Atlantic islands, as their next destination. The archipelago was known for its stunning lakes, volcanic craters, natural reserves, botanical gardens, and pink-sand beaches. Several residents asked why they couldn't choose the destinations themselves, and Charlotte had to resist rolling her eyes at the notion. Who knew where they might end up? Probably Ittoqqortoormiit, Greenland, eating caviar made of whale blubber.

The fact was (and Charlotte explained this in detail), they needed a week to restock the food, liquor, and other supplies; double-check the equipment, route, and itinerary; and take into consideration the weather forecasts for the coming weeks. Not to mention that luxury hotel and guided-tour reservations must be made weeks, sometimes months, in advance.

Of course, these behind-the-scenes preparations never occurred to the residents who were used to having all their needs catered to without ever lifting a finger. Charlotte called them the "bubble people" because they lived such charmed, insulated lives. Naturally, she kept these thoughts to herself. She was, after all, the image of professionalism.

Leaning her arms on the railing, she thought back on the Savannah Seas maiden voyage, which almost didn't happen because the owners had embezzled all the money. They dodged a bullet, but that was next? Hitting an iceberg? A pirate attack at sea? Norovirus running rampant

on board? She planned for every possibility throughout her career, but that embezzlement business took her by surprise.

Another name for a ship's captain was "master," and Charlotte also thought of herself as a director, conductor, and one-person steering committee. The 250 millionaires and billionaires on board might be out seeing the world, but her job was to keep them safely in their bubbles. Was she equal to the task? You bet.

So, why couldn't she calm the feeling of rough waters ahead?

It's Review Time

Please leave a review. It would mean so much to me. I wanted to share this story about real women who never give up. Who do you know needs inspiration on how to live life?

Good or bad, I want to hear from you. All it takes is one little sentence, more is good too. I just want to know if you were inspired by this story.

Go to Amazon.com and search for Savannah Seas by Cynthia Manion.

Thank you sincerely

About Cynthia Manion

My mission is to reach humans over 55 years of age who may have lost themselves along the life path.

I want to bring joy and caring to others, and I do this through my books, speeches, acting and personal appearances.

The daughter of an Air Force Lieutenant Colonel and a homemaker, Cynthia developed her "people skills" at an early age.

Her father's military obligations dictated that her family continually move while growing up.

Cynthia resided in Europe, East Africa and the Seychelles Islands. Upon her father's retirement, the family settled in suburban Washington, D.C.

At age 15, Cynthia began modeling. She was booked into conventions, print ads and onto runways for clients Such as Ford Aerospace, Bordens, May Co, Colt 45 and Black Label beers among others. Cynthia recalled, "When I first started out, I modeled as a Hoola girl, cowgirl, foot soldier and even an astronaut."

In 1978 she graduated with honors with an Associate degree from Mt. Vernon College Washington D.C. then decided to further her education when she was admitted into Georgetown University.

When she was 21 her mother died of leukemia and Cynthia decided to leave school to care for her two younger sisters ages three and fourteen and her sixteen-year-old brother. As she soon discovered, taking care of a family was not as easy as her mother had made it look, but the challenge helping raise her family contributed significantly to her strength of character.

Several years later when Cynthia's father remarried, she could once again concentrate on her own life.

To establish her independence and to pursue a career in modeling, 23-year-old Cynthia moved to New York City with a mattress strapped to the top of her car and $450 in her pocket. She found an apartment for $400 and after assessing her finances, she realized she had less than three weeks to find a job.

With a copy of The Ross Reports in hand (a booklet listing modeling contacts) Cynthia remembers "I went through that book alphabetically and pounded the pavement for 2 1/2 weeks in high heels before landing my first job."

Her career began to flourish modeling for Oscar de la Renta and Serena Swimwear.

In addition to modeling, Cynthia's career as an actress took off when she started appearing in popular soap operas

including *As the World Turns, Loving and One Life to Live*, as well as feature films such as *Desperately Seeking Susan, Girls Night Out, Preppies, Blowout,* and *Diner.*

She has also graced the covers of national magazines including *Motor Boat and Sailing* and *Baltimore Magazine* among others.

In 1986 Cynthia's life took a new turn. She had always had an interest in business and what started out as a modeling assignment for Gloria Vanderbilt turned into a new opportunity.

Cynthia moved into the sales end of the business and was eventually named national sales manager for the company.

Cynthia's aptitude for business served her well when Harley Davidson placed her in charge of their national merchandising.

During this time, she also produced and directed fashion shows for Cotler Men's Wear.

In 1988 she married and in 1991 became a mother.

Cynthia had it all. However once again her emotional strength would be put to the test.

During the holidays in 1991, Cynthia shattered her leg in a skiing accident. The injury was so severe that doctors warned her she might not walk normally again.

Cynthia couldn't walk for eight months and for three of those months it was a struggle for her to sit upright.

"In order to repair my leg, the surgeon utilized a

five-hole metal plate, five screws, two washers and scooped out a cup of bone from my hip to fill it in with. I really felt like a bionic woman," remembers Cynthia.

She devoted 18 months to physical therapy. "I remember looking at my little boy and thinking how much I wanted to be able to run and play with him - I did everything and more to strengthen my leg," recalls Cynthia. As she began to recover, she focused on a new goal deciding to compete for the title of "Mrs. New York America."

A lot of people over 55 have lost their dreams, I am here to bring a little joy and open you to becoming who you really want to be, NOW!

www.ingramcontent.com/pod-product-compliance
Lightning Source LLC
Chambersburg PA
CBHW051513260626
47162CB00008B/2955